All In

a M/M erotic romance

by Alexa Land

Book Two in the Firsts and Forever Series

Dedicated to Frankie

my first fan-boy :)

Contents

6

Chapter One

"Dude, if you keep staring at the boss like that, you're going to get fired. That is, if you're lucky."

I glanced at Cole and asked, "And if I'm not lucky?"

"Then his mafia husband is going to put a bullet in your brain and toss your body in a dumpster," my coworker said as he stuffed a backpack in his locker.

"His husband isn't in the mafia anymore. Besides, he was never that kind of gangster," I pointed out as I snuck another look at Jamie, my ex-boyfriend. He and his new husband Dmitri were deep in conversation in their office, arms around each other, foreheads touching. It was painful as hell to watch. And yet, my gaze kept drifting to them.

"So, you think you retire from the mob and suddenly forget how to off the competition?"

I sighed and turned my back to the office, peeling off my grey t-shirt. "I'm hardly the competition."

"You and Jamie were together for eight years, right? And you broke up, what, six months ago? You really think his husband isn't threatened by that kind of history, or by a guy who looks like you do?"

"I really don't think a man as good-looking as Dmitri would find anything whatsoever threatening about me."

Cole made a show of running his gaze slowly down my bare torso. Then he said sarcastically, "Oh yeah, who'd feel threatened by a six-two jock with abs you could chip a tooth on?" He slapped my stomach playfully, and I rolled my eyes. "Look Charlie, just play it cool around those two, okay? I like working with you, and it'd suck if you got yourself fired. Or dead."

"Yeah, okay. I'll work on that." I gave him a little half-smile.

My coworker grinned at me, his brown eyes sparkling behind his glasses as he tied an apron around his hips. "Good. Now hurry up, beefcake. The bar opens in ten minutes," he said as he left the employee dressing room.

Just because I was an idiot, I snuck another look at Jamie and Dmitri over my shoulder. They were kissing, deeply, tenderly. It made my heart ache, especially because it reminded me of the way they'd kissed each other when they'd gotten married just a few weeks ago.

The wedding had been on the beach at sunset. Jamie was a life-long surfer and the ocean was a part of him, so the location was perfect. They'd said they wanted to keep it small and simple, but there'd still been about a hundred guests witnessing the joyous union (for those two, that was actually just immediate family and closest friends). The ceremony was beautiful and romantic. I must have been out of my mind for attending.

I pulled on my dark green work t-shirt and tucked it into my Levis. The name of the bar was emblazoned in white letters across my chest. It said *Nolan's*. That was such rich irony. I *had*, in fact, at one time belonged to Jamie Nolan. But then I'd gotten scared and ran from the relationship. It was the biggest mistake of my life.

Now every day, I came to work in my ex's bar and wore this shirt with his name on it. Every day I got to feel the full impact of my loss, over and over and over again. And every day I got to remind myself that this pain was totally self-inflicted. I broke up with him because I was too scared to accept my sexuality, to come out to my family and friends, to admit to myself just how much Jamie meant to me, until it was too late. I would never again, despite the declaration on my shirt, be Jamie Nolan's.

And it was all. My. Fault.

I tied my black apron around my hips and took a look in the mirror beside the lockers. After a quick finger-comb of my short, dark brown hair and a frown at the bloodshot condition of my green eyes, I went out to the dining room. Cole was topping off the salt shakers, and as I got busy doing the same thing with the pepper, he asked, "So, speaking of gangsters, are you still planning to go out with that Sicilian stereotype?"

On impulse, I'd accepted a date last week with a guy I'd met at the bar. His name was Dante Dombruso, and I actually didn't realize until sometime later that he was some sort of mafia heavy hitter. Okay, I didn't so much *realize* it as have it yelled in my face by a panicked Jamie when I'd mentioned I was going out with Dante. Totally hypocritical, if you ask me. His husband had only recently broken away from the Russian mafia, after all.

"I don't know what's going on with that. He's cancelled on me twice, both times on short notice," I told Cole.

"Were you actually interested in him?" my coworker asked, as he poured a steady stream of salt into a little glass shaker with a flourish. I shrugged noncommittally, even though the answer to that question was a resounding *yes*.

Dante Dombruso was exactly what I needed to get over Jamie. He was six feet, four inches of raw temptation and hard Italian muscle, wrapped in an expensive suit. Whatever my personal hang-ups were, they somehow didn't matter when I was near him. My body responded to him on a primal level, and my brain just went along for the ride.

I'd been sure of two things: Dante Dombruso wanted to fuck me, and I wanted to let him. It was so straightforward, so uncomplicated. The perfect rebound fling. But then he broke two dates with me, which threw off the straightforward and uncomplicated part a bit.

Cole studied me for a long moment. I'd been working at the bar only a week, but I'd known him for a while. I'd been a regular at this establishment since turning twenty-one two years ago, and he'd worked here about that long. But back when I was a customer it was called Flannigan's, it wasn't owned by my ex, and my life hadn't totally been in the crapper. He said, "So, you know, maybe Dombruso cancelling on you is a sign. Maybe the universe is trying to intervene and keep you from making a big mistake."

"Since when does the universe care about me making mistakes?"

Speaking of which, my ex came into the dining room, looking adorably tousled and a little flushed. God. "Hi guys," he said to Cole and me as he crossed the room to unlock the front door and flip on the neon sign that declared the bar and grill open.

"Hey," I mumbled, turning my back to him as I got really interested in the pepper shakers.

A moment later, I felt a light touch on my arm and glanced at Jamie. Concern was evident in his sky blue eyes as he asked, "How are you, Charlie?"

Depressed. Lonely. Missing you like crazy. "Fine," I said, looking away again and screwing the lid back on a pepper shaker.

He hadn't removed his hand from my arm. "How are you really?" he asked gently.

I hated this, I hated the be-nice-to poor-fucked-up-Charlie routine. It made me feel even more pathetic than I already did. I met his gaze and said steadily, "I'm fine, thanks."

Instead of removing his hand, he rubbed my upper arm. His touch was so sweet and tender that he might as well have just gone ahead and punched me in the face. It was that painful a reminder of all I'd lost. He said, "You know you can talk to me, right? You're going through a lot right now, and I want you to know I'm here for you."

He didn't mean our break-up. Last week, I'd finally come out to my parents. As a result, I'd gotten kicked out of the house I grew up in. I was now subletting a kind of depressing empty apartment Jamie had recently vacated.

"I know, and I appreciate it, Jamie." I broke eye contact again. He was so close to me that I breathed in his scent. Jamie always smelled a little like the ocean and like clean cotton. Now he also smelled faintly of his new husband's expensive cologne, which made me feel like whacking my head against a wall. "I've got to finish setting up my station. I'll talk to you later, okay?" I turned my back to him and pulled a dish towel from my apron, wiping up some of the pepper I'd spilled.

"Okay, Charlie." He paused a moment before finally going back to his office. As soon as he was out of sight, I bent over and thunked my head against the table in front of me, then just stayed there for a while, wrapping my arms around my head.

Coming to work here had been *such* a stupid idea. Jamie, in his ongoing effort to save me from myself, had offered me the job so I could end the nightmare of working for my uncle's exterminator business. It was a great bar, but God, the Jamie factor was just so hard to take.

Being here was somewhat bearable when the place was busy and I had less time to wallow. But Jamie was trying out something new by opening the bar for lunch, and these daytime shifts had been so quiet you could hear crickets chirping. It would probably pick up when word got out that we were open this time of day, but that hadn't happened yet.

Besides the not entirely successful lunchtime experiment, the bar and grill business was going great for my ex and his husband. Nights and weekends were hopping. They'd started running this place just a few weeks ago, and the change in ownership had made it more popular than ever. I wouldn't have predicted that. Even a city as famously liberal as San Francisco still had a conservative element, and I hadn't expected the patrons of an Irish sports bar to stick around when the place was taken over by a gay ex-cop and his ex-mafia husband. But not only had the blue collars stayed, they'd slid over and made room for the influx of young urban hipsters that suddenly found something appealing about this place, ever since locally famous former gangster and former nightclub owner Dmitri Teplov became associated with it.

Although apparently, neither the hipsters nor the blue collars had gotten the come-and-get-drunk-on-your-lunch-break memo.

I was still bent over the table, face down and trying to find the motivation to actually get up, when a deep voice behind me said, "Well, that right there made the trip across town totally worth it." I raised my head and peered over my shoulder, and there was Dante Dombruso, arms crossed over his chest, a big grin on his face as he studied my upturned ass.

I stood up quickly, and in the process I knocked over the large carton of pepper that I'd left on the table. I actually caught it as it fell, but on the upswing I managed to fling some directly into my face. Did you know pepper actually makes you sneeze? *A lot.* And here I'd thought that was only in cartoons. I sneezed about five times in as many seconds, and Dante held something out to me.

A-choo! "Seriously?" I asked, both hands over my nose and mouth as I squinted at the pristine, monogrammed square of fabric he was holding out to me. *A-choo!*

"Yes. Take the handkerchief."

A-choo! "Do you honestly expect me—" *A-choo!* "—to blow my nose in that and then hand it back to you?" *A-choo!* "Because that's super weird and gross."

He grinned at that and said, "Keep it."

A-choo! "Okay. Thanks." I grabbed the handkerchief and blew my nose loudly and inelegantly. It actually helped tremendously, and I sighed with relief as the sneezing ceased. Then I said, "I've never understood cloth handkerchiefs. The only logical thing to do once you've covered something with snot is throw it away."

"So your argument against cloth handkerchiefs is that they're illogical?" Dante looked highly amused by all of this.

"No, my argument against cloth handkerchiefs is that the moment you use them, they become a totally repulsive snot vault that you're supposed to keep in your pocket. I don't even know what to do with this now." I held the article in question away from me with two fingers.

"I would offer to take it back, but you've made such a compelling argument about its total repulsiveness that I now want nothing to do with it."

"See? I'm going to wash it out in the restroom. It's the only thing I can think of to do with this," I said, and crossed the empty dining room.

Dante actually followed me into the restroom, and I lobbed the handkerchief into the sink and ran hot water over it. When I turned to face him, he grinned and said, "Hi."

"Hello, Dante."

"You're mad at me," he observed, resting against the door.

"Mildly annoyed." I leaned against the counter opposite him and studied him carefully. Dante was tall, muscular and classically handsome. He had jet black, longish hair and olive skin, and a slightly prominent nose offset by smoldering dark brown eyes and full lips. He wore a black-on-black-on-black impeccably tailored suit, shirt, and tie, and had apparently spent all of his adult life perfecting the five o'clock shadow, which he had down to an art form.

"I'm sorry for breaking our date."

"Twice."

"Twice," he confirmed.

"Are you here to make and break a third?"

"I'm here to make and *keep* a third, if you're willing to give me another chance."

"I have to be honest with you, Dante," I said, crossing my arms over my chest. "I can't handle a whole lot of personal rejection at this particular point in my life. So please only ask me out if you fully intend to show up this time."

"For what it's worth, I have a really good excuse for breaking those dates."

"Don't tell me, let me guess. Sick grandmother?"

I'd been being sarcastic, coming up with the most clichéd excuse I could think of, but his eyes went wide at that and he said, "That's exactly right. How did you know?"

I assumed he was kidding, and rolled my eyes. "Funny."

Dante crossed the small room to me and turned off the water in the sink (which had been about to overflow), then leaned against the counter right beside me, so close our arms were touching. He pulled out his phone and scrolled though his text messages, then handed it to me. The message on the screen said that his grandmother had suffered a heart attack, and instructed Dante to come to the hospital immediately. The text was from last Thursday, when we were supposed to have our first date.

Now I felt like a total and complete asshole for joking about sick grandmothers, and I murmured, "God, I'm sorry," as I handed his phone back to him. "Is she okay?"

"Thanks. She's doing a lot better. She'd started to take a turn for the worse Saturday. That's when I cancelled the second date you and I had scheduled. But yesterday and today, she's really come around, so I figured I could break away and come see you."

"You should've told me sooner that this was why you were cancelling," I said as I looked up at him.

"Would you really have believed me if I'd told you I was breaking our date because of a sick grandmother?"

"I…might have." *Hell no, absolutely not.*

He grinned at that, and then he pivoted around so he had me pinned to the counter, one of his thighs lightly pressing against mine. Dante whispered, his lips right beside my ear, "Please give me another chance, Charlie."

I suddenly remembered so very clearly why I'd agreed to go out with Dante in the first place. My entire body responded to his proximity, my heart pounding and all the blood rushing from my brain to my cock, making me feel slightly lightheaded. He was so far out of my comfort zone that I couldn't even *see* my comfort zone from there. But somehow, it didn't matter. When I got close to him, my libido took over and I was able to just go with it.

Usually, sex scared the hell out of me. I'd never gotten farther than oral with my ex in the eight years we'd dated. But I felt certain this could happen with Dante, both because I knew he was the type of man to totally take charge and guide me through it, and because of my new mantra: *fear isn't a valid excuse.*

I had let fear shape my life for so long, and so profoundly, up to and including letting it convince me to break up with Jamie. Fear had cost me everything, and now I was absolutely determined to stop letting it dictate my decisions. In fact, I'd decided to embrace the things that frightened me. If something was scary, I was absolutely going to do it anyway.

"Okay. When do you want to go out?" I asked as casually as I could, as if I wasn't about to suffer a hard-on induced stroke.

"How about tonight?" He was still really close to me, and his big hands came up and traced a light path down my arms.

I started to sink into him, letting lust be my guide. But then I remembered something and pulled back abruptly as I said, "Shit. I can't tonight, there's something I need to do."

"You're still mad at me."

"No, that's not it. There really is something I have to do tonight."

"Can I do it with you?"

That kind of surprised me. "You have no idea what you're volunteering for," I pointed out.

"I know. But whatever it is, I'm up for it."

"Are you trying to be extra agreeable to make up for the broken dates?"

"Yup," he said with a grin. "Will you let me join you?"

"Yeah, okay." I actually really liked the idea of having someone along for the night I had planned.

"So, what have I gotten myself into?"

I smiled at him cheerfully. "Nothing much. Just a little felony breaking and entering."

Chapter Two

He'd totally thought I was kidding.

I met him in front of my apartment that evening at seven sharp and he started to escort me to his car, but I said, "I'll drive. We're going to need my truck for this."

"For what?"

"For the breaking and entering. Or you know, the part of breaking and entering where we haul away our bounty. Your BMW is too small for the job."

"So, you were actually serious about that?" Dante stared at me incredulously.

"I never kid about committing felonies," I told him with mock-seriousness, then swung open the passenger door of my truck for him.

Instead of getting in, he paused right in front of me. He was fighting back a smile, and tried to look grave as he said, "Have you committed a lot of felonies?"

"Nope, this is my first. But I'm highly prepared. I Googled breaking and entering and found out everything I need to know. Plus, now I have you along as a crime consultant." I flashed a big, toothy grin at him.

"So you know what I do for a living."

"Yes. Granted, bringing you along for this is kind of like bringing a tank into a knife fight. But still, I'll bet your expertise will come in handy. For one thing, you might know how to work these." I pulled a little black and white case out of the pocket of my jeans and held it up.

"What is that?"

"It's a lock picking kit."

"Is that...my God, it is. It's got Hello Kitty on it." He burst out laughing.

"Yeah, yeah," I said, rolling my eyes. "I know it's not the big, manly lock picking set you're probably used to in your line of work. But this one was half as expensive as any of the others."

"Where does one even find a Hello Kitty lock picking kit?" Dante asked with a raised eyebrow and a huge smile.

"eBay, of course. You can find *anything* on eBay."

"Apparently."

"Get in," I said, "We're burning moonlight."

He plucked the little case from my hand and got in the truck. I slammed his door (three times, because it had a tendency to swing open unexpectedly if you didn't close it just right), and then went around and got behind the wheel. As I fired up the engine and pulled away from the curb, Dante unzipped the kit and pulled out a couple slender tools.

"These seem pretty flimsy," he pointed out, bending one of the tools slightly with his thumb. "They probably wouldn't pick anything sturdier than a typical residential lock."

"Well, then it's a damn good thing we're not headed to the Wells Fargo Bank right now."

"No? That's too bad. I haven't pulled a good bank job in weeks." I glanced over at him and he grinned and said, "Kidding." He turned around in his seat a bit and studied my profile as he asked, "Are you actually okay with my job? You really seem to be taking it in stride, far better than I would have anticipated."

The mafia thing was utterly bizarre to me, something so far removed from the world I lived in that I couldn't even sort of come to grips with it. So I'd compartmentalized it, tucked it away for later analysis. Instead of trying to explain that, I answered with another question. "Are you really okay with me taking you to commit a felony on our first date? Because most people would find that odd."

"Oh, I find it incredibly odd," he said, "and also completely entertaining. I don't date a lot, but I'm pretty sure this first date is already totally off the charts in terms of overall bizarreness."

"Don't worry, there will be time for a normal date after the breaking and entering. We can grab some dinner if you want, and then go back to my apartment for loads of wild monkey sex." I had to say that humorously, because if I'd said it any other way, I might have induced a panic attack in myself.

"Works for me," he said cheerfully, and rested his big hand on my right thigh.

A couple minutes later, I parked the car on a quiet residential street in the Richmond and took a deep breath. I'd been trying to keep this little excursion light and upbeat, but my nerves surfaced now and I gripped the steering wheel tightly. I stalled for a long moment, leaning forward to look at a white house up the street. If I hadn't brought a date, I really might have bailed on this whole thing and gone back home. But having Dante along made me feel a little more confident about this whole endeavor, for some reason.

I took another deep breath, then swung the door open. "Please grab that white bag by your feet and bring it along," I said as I got out of the truck.

He did as I asked, peeking into the fast food sack he carried as we walked down the sidewalk. "What's this for?"

"It's to distract Peaches."

"What's Peaches?"

"You'll see." I jogged across the street with Dante right behind me, then hesitated at the foot of the staircase leading up to the simple, white, row house. I sighed and said as I looked up at the front door, "This is going to be pretty anticlimactic if they're home."

"Want me to go up and knock on the door?" Dante asked.

"That's a good idea. I'll wait over here," I said, and ducked around the side of the staircase.

He jogged up the stairs and knocked on the front door, which instantly triggered a barking frenzy inside the house. After a few moments he tried the bell, and the barking grew even louder. But no one came to the door.

"Looks like we're good to go." I climbed the stairs, took my lock picking kit from Dante, and crouched down as I said, "You be the lookout. I watched a YouTube video on how to do this. It should only take a minute." I unzipped the case and removed two of the tools.

"Are you ever going to tell me whose house this is?" Dante asked, turning his back to the door and watching the street.

"Walter and Ida Connolly's," I said.

"And who are Walter and Ida Connolly?"

"My parents."

"We're robbing your parents?"

"Noooo. That'd be nuts. We're just going to get some of my stuff. We're leaving their stuff alone."

"I don't understand. Why is your stuff locked up in your parents' house, and why do we need to break in to get it?"

I jiggled the tools in the shiny new lock as I said, "Up until last week, I lived here. Then I came out to my parents, and was disowned on the spot. That of course also included getting kicked out. I'd only had the foresight to pack up some clothes beforehand and stash them in my truck. I just thought I'd have to clear out for a couple days until they calmed down a bit. I totally underestimated the full extent of their rabid, Bible-thumping bigotry."

"I'm sorry, Charlie."

I sighed and said, "It is what it is. I should have anticipated this and planned ahead. But instead, stupidly, I gave them more credit than they deserved. Damn, this lock picking kit isn't working."

"Do you want me to try?"

"Sure." We traded places, and I took over the job of lookout.

While Dante went to work on the lock, I said, "I tried to come back home toward the end of last week, which was when I realized they'd changed the locks. My father swore at me through the door and told me I wasn't welcome here anymore. He told me never to come back. That's fine with me, except for the fact that everything I own is locked up in that house, and I'd like at least some of it back." I fought to keep my voice steady through that, mustering all my bravado.

"What if they got rid of your stuff?" Dante was still working diligently on the lock.

"I guess that's a possibility. I would have come sooner, but they're always home. This is the one night of the week I knew they'd be gone, because this is when they play bridge with the Sullivans." I turned to see how Dante was doing, and told him, "They'll be home in less than two hours, so could you step it up a bit?"

Dante stood up and said, "Yeah, I totally can't pick that lock."

"You can't?"

"Nope."

"How is that even possible?" I asked him.

He smirked at me and put the lock picking kit in my hand. "I've never picked a lock in my life."

"You're kidding."

"Why would I have done this?"

"Um, because you're in the mafia?"

"I'm in the *real* mafia, not the *Kindergarten* mafia. If you want me to shoot the lock out, that I can do."

I raised an eyebrow at him. "Are you armed right now?"

"Do you want me to shoot the lock?"

"Hell no! Attracting the attention of the whole neighborhood with gunfire would be highly counterproductive. So does that mean you *are* armed right now?"

"Do you really want to know?" He was grinning at me, his dark eyes sparkling.

I thought about it for a moment, then said, "No. Come on, let's try the back door."

As we walked around the block to get to the alley behind my parents' house, Dante took my hand. I visibly flinched a little when he did that, so he asked, "Are you okay with holding hands?"

"Yeah. I mean, I'm not really used to public displays of affection. I only came out last week, remember? Before that, I was way, *way* in the closet. Like, back there with the winter coats and old prom dresses. But, you know, I need to get used to being out."

"If it makes you uncomfortable, you can always let go of me," he said, giving my hand a gentle squeeze.

I tightened my grip on him and said, "No thank you."

When we got to the alley, I jiggled the back gate and found it locked as usual. I paused for a moment and regarded the seven foot high wooden fence with my hands on my hips. Then I dragged over a lidded trash can, climbed on top of it, and looked down at Dante. "I can't believe you wore a three thousand dollar suit tonight. Didn't I tell you we'd be breaking and entering?"

He grinned up at me. "You did. I didn't believe you."

I hopped onto the top of the fence and sat on it for a moment. "You can wait there if you want. It'd be a shame to mess up a suit that cost more than my truck."

"No way am I sitting this out," Dante said, removing his suit jacket and slinging it onto the top of the fence beside me. He rolled back his sleeves as he said, "Speaking of that piece of shit you drive, would you be offended if I bought you a new car?"

"What? Yes!"

He got up on the trash can and I jumped into the yard. He then climbed onto the top of the fence somewhat awkwardly and balanced precariously for a moment. Finally he caught his balance and leapt into the yard, landing right in front of me. "This is fun," he said. "I don't remember the last time I hopped a fence."

I grinned at that. "Probably because you're not in the Kindergarten mafia."

"Probably." He smiled at me, and drew me into his arms.

"What are you doing?"

"Thinking about kissing you."

"Why?"

"Why?" He echoed incredulously.

"I mean, why now? Did hopping a fence make you randy?"

He laughed at that. "No. Well...kind of. Do you really call it being randy?"

"The word 'horny' is kinda gross if you think about it. I immediately picture a big frog with horns on its head. You know, like a horny toad? Either that, or I think of Austin Powers, saying, *do I make you hoooorny?*" I'd said that last part with a British accent, of course. Then I added, "Ew."

"God, you're bizarre," Dante said with a big smile, still holding me in his arms. It was pretty dark in the backyard, but his amused expression was unmistakable.

"But don't you agree that horny is kind of a gross word?"

"No. Are you rambling like this because the thought of kissing me makes you nervous?"

"Definitely."

"Thought so," he said, before brushing his lips to mine.

I wrapped my arms around him and held on tight as the kiss deepened and my lips parted under his. My entire body responded as the kiss became passionate, insistent, his tongue claiming my mouth, his big hands crushing me against him. Everything else fell away, besides Dante, and me, and that epic kiss.

Then the dog started barking inside the house, bringing me back to the here and now. It brought Dante back to earth, too. He picked up my hand and we went around to the kitchen door on the right side of the building.

I crouched down and went to work on the lock. There was a little light coming from the neighbor's house, just enough to see by. Dante pulled his phone out of his pocket, and as he flipped through a few screens he said, "Randy is far worse than horny. Unless you're British, I suppose. But since I'm not British, the word Randy immediately conjures images of a guy with a big belt buckle who drives a truck."

"Truck drivers with big belt buckles make you randy?"

"No! Truck drivers with big belt buckles would be *called* Randy. The proper noun, not the adjective you're trying to make it into."

"It's an adjective? Not a verb?"

"Why would randy be a verb?" Dante asked as he crouched down beside me.

"I dunno. Seems like an action word."

He chuckled at that and held up his phone, then tapped the screen. A YouTube video on lock picking started to play. I studied the video, then concentrated on the lock. Fifteen minutes later, I sat back on my heels and sighed. "I suck at this."

"Here, let me try," Dante said, and we traded places. I played the video for him again and he watched closely, then went to work on the lock.

"Maybe I should have spent more money and not gone with the Hello Kitty lock pick set," I said after a while.

"Ya think?"

"So maybe we should come back same time next week with some better tools."

"Oh, there's nothing wrong with these tools," Dante said, his brow knit in concentration as he worked the lock. "You just shouldn't have gotten the Hello Kitty set because you're a grown man, and not a five-year-old girl."

I laughed at that. "What kind of a psychotic company would make a lock pick set for a five-year-old girl?"

"What, do you think *you're* the target market for that product?"

"Apparently, since I actually bought it."

"Incidentally, I'm pretty sure that kit isn't a licensed Sanrio product," he informed me. "The cat doesn't look quite right. Its head's kind of square. It's probably some sort of cheap, trademark violating knockoff. Not so much Hello Kitty as Hell No Kitty."

I laughed at that. "Well, I'll be sure to turn 'em in to the Hello Kitty police. Why do you know that the company that makes Hello Kitty is Sanrio?"

"Everyone knows that. Come here and help me."

I crouched down beside him. "What do you want me to do?"

"Kiss me," he said, and leaned over and planted a big smooch on my lips. He smiled at me and added, "Now hold this bottom tool in place while I work the top one."

After a couple minutes with both of us working on it, we heard a clicking sound and looked at each other with wide eyes. Dante reached up and turned the door handle. "It's unlocked," he said with a huge smile.

"We did it!"

"Well, either that or it was unlocked the whole time. I don't think we actually checked it before we started working on it."

"No, think positive," I said, straightening up. "We're awesome. We totally picked the hell out of that lock."

Dante straightened up too, and we gave each other a high-five. He reached for the door handle, and I said, "Get the hamburgers ready."

"The what?'

"The hamburgers. Wait, what did you do with the fast food bag?"

"Shit. I must have left it on the front porch."

"Oh man! How are you even a criminal? *I'm* a better criminal than you are!"

Dante chuckled at that. "Want me to go back over the fence and around to the front of the house and grab the bag?"

"No. It'll take way too long, and this has already taken forever. We're going in, just stay behind me. I'm going to go straight through to the front door and grab the burgers, and then when we've used them to distract Peaches we can run upstairs to my room and get my stuff. We're not going to try to take everything, just a few clothes and a couple things that have sentimental value," I told him. Then I flung the kitchen door open.

We were greeted by a small, brownish-black spiky mess of fur with big sharp teeth and a tremendous underbite. It growled and lunged and snapped viciously. "My God, what is that?" Dante asked, slipping into the kitchen and closing the door behind us. He really did stay behind me, using me as a human shield. Chicken.

"That's Peaches."

"But...what is it?"

"It's a dog."

"That's not a dog," Dante said as he leapt back a few inches, out of snapping underbite range.

"Sure it is. What else would it be?" I asked as I carefully eased around the crazed canine.

"A rabid, reanimated Muppet, maybe? What the hell kind of dog is it?"

"He's an Affenpinscher. Mostly."

"That's not a real breed," Dante said, hugging the wall behind me as I guided us through the kitchen and down the hall.

"Of course it is." The dog continued to snarl and jump at us. He made up for the fact that he was only a foot tall by his hell-bent determination to kill us.

"Wait! You lived here, up until a week ago. Why is it attacking you?"

"Peaches has always hated me." We'd finally reached the front door, and I swung it open carefully, holding the dog back with my foot. "Actually, he hates everyone, except for my mom and dad."

The dog growled and latched onto the cuff of my jeans, shaking his head violently, as if he was trying to kill my foot like a rat. "Oh shit," Dante exclaimed. "It's got you. Want me to shoot it?"

"Hell no, I don't want you to shoot my parents' dog! Though if you'd remembered the hamburgers, *that* would have been helpful."

"You didn't remember them either."

"You were carrying the bag. It was your responsibility," I said as I hopped up and down on one foot, the eleven-pound dog trying his damnedest to pull me off balance, and reached outside the door and grabbed the white paper bag.

I thrust the sack at Dante. "Throw him a hamburger. That'll distract him." The dog was still shaking my pant leg violently, and Dante grabbed a burger, pulled off the paper, and started to throw it to Peaches. "Not the bun," I told him, holding onto the doorframe with both hands to keep from tipping over.

"Why not?" he asked as he shook the patty onto the floor. Immediately, the dog let go of my leg and started scarfing down the meat.

I stood upright and pushed my hair off my forehead as I said, "Because Peaches has a gluten intolerance. If he eats bread, he'll have diarrhea for a week."

Dante stared at me for a long moment with one eyebrow raised, as if I was totally insane. Then, while still maintaining eye contact with me, he tossed the bun to the dog. Peaches caught it and wolfed it down.

"Shame on you," I said, crossing my arms and frowning at Dante.

"That thing deserves some intestinal distress. Hell, it deserves a bullet in the cranium. Shooting it would be a public service."

The dog started to growl again, and I said, "Quick, throw him another burger. *No bun* this time."

He rolled his eyes and did as I asked. I locked the front door and turned to head up the stairs. But something caught my eye, and I paused for a moment. "What's wrong?" Dante wanted to know.

"Um...nothing. There just...well, there used to be pictures of me all along the wall here, going up the staircase, from when I was growing up. My parents took them all down. But whatever." I felt like I'd just been kicked in the gut, but no way was I going to make a big deal out of it in front of my date. It was already embarrassing enough that I was involving him in my little family drama.

"Shit. I'm sorry."

"It's fine," I lied, and jogged up the stairs. Dante was right behind me, but had to pause long enough to throw more beef at Peaches when the dog started to growl and follow us.

I got to my room at the end of the hall, opened the door and flipped the light switch. I totally froze in my tracks. The room was bare. The only things left in it were the stripped-down mattress and an empty desk. The closet was open, and that was empty, too. The room looked small and stark and barren, with blank rectangles on the faded blue walls where my posters had once been. "Damn it," I murmured. "We're too late."

Dante threw another patty to the dog, then stepped into the empty room with me and shut the door behind us. "Fuck, that sucks. I'm so sorry, Charlie."

I started to tell him it was fine, but the words wouldn't form in my mouth. I looked around at my former home, at the room that had been mine for twenty-three years. I swallowed hard against the lump in my throat, the pain raw, searing, and took a few deep breaths. Dante took my hand and held on tight, wordlessly, just giving me a minute. Eventually I said, "We have to get out of here, my parents will be home soon. This is all bad enough without also getting hauled to jail for breaking and entering."

Peaches was waiting patiently in the hall, and as soon as I opened the door, he stood up and started growling again. Dante reached into the bag and tossed the dog all the buns he'd been saving. When he saw my disapproving expression, he said, "Your parents totally deserve a giant case of explosive diarrhea. They deserve far, far worse than that, actually."

"That's just mean," I told him, shutting off the overhead light in my room and pulling the door shut behind me.

"I don't have a problem with mean," Dante said as he jogged down the stairs after me.

We left through the kitchen door since my parents were likely to pull up to the front of the house at any moment, and locked it behind us. We made it outside without incident, because Peaches was still busy giving himself diarrhea. When we reached the back fence, both of us laced our fingers together and bent down to give the other a boost. "Go ahead," he said.

"No, you go ahead," I told him, still in position to give him a leg up.

Dante straightened up and said, fists on his hips, the paper bag still clutched in one hand, "I can make it over this fence without assistance, thank you very much."

"No you can't. You barely made it over with the aid of a trash can."

He laughed at that and said indignantly, "That is *not* true."

"It *is* true," I teased. "Plus, at your advanced age, you might break a hip or something. So come on, Dombruso, take the leg up." I still held my hands laced together for him.

"Advanced age! How old do you think I am?"

"I dunno. Twenty-eight, twenty-nine?"

He grinned at me and said, "That's actually right. I'm twenty-nine. Still young enough to do this." He turned from me and tossed the fast food bag over the fence before pulling himself up gracefully. When he was sitting on the top of the fence, he looked down at me with a smug expression and said, "See?"

"If you can do that, why was it so hard to jump over the fence in the first place?"

"I was out of practice." Something caught Dante's eye, and he turned his head to the left, squinting into the darkness. "Hey, what do you suppose is in all those bags over there?"

I turned to look, and only then noticed about a dozen big, black garbage bags lined up along the edge of the yard. I jogged over to them, untangled one of the drawstrings, and took a look inside. "Holy crap, this is some of my stuff," I exclaimed. I checked another bag and announced, "So's this. I guess my parents hadn't gotten around to hauling it to the dump yet."

He smiled at that. "So, in other words, we just spent all that time breaking into your parents' house and facing off against the zombie lap dog from hell for absolutely no reason."

"Yeah, pretty much," I said, carrying a couple bags over to the back gate. "Out of curiosity, how do you figure Peaches is a zombie?"

"It smells like it's rotting."

"That's just his breath. He won't let anyone brush his teeth, not even my mom." I handed the bags up to him as I said, "Could you please lower these to the other side? I don't know what's breakable in here, so I don't just want to chuck them over."

When we got the eleven bags up and over the fence, Dante jumped into the alley, pulling his suit jacket down with him. When I climbed over the fence and landed in front of him, he kissed the tip of my nose, then went back to rolling down his sleeves and buttoning his cuffs.

"I'm going to bring my truck around. Could you please stay here and keep an eye on my stuff?" I asked him.

"Sure."

When I pulled up beside him a couple minutes later, Dante pointed his phone's screen at me and said, "Turns out 'Affenpinscher' is a real breed." A picture of a small, black, apelike dog was on the screen. "Did you know 'aff' means monkey in German?"

"I told you so. And yes, I did actually know that. Peaches isn't a purebred, though. We don't really know what else he is, since he was an unclaimed stray that my parents got at the pound."

"Imagine that, such a sweet animal going unclaimed," Dante deadpanned as he put his phone away and hoisted a couple bags into the bed of my pickup.

"It was my fault they got him in the first place. I pestered them to get a dog for years. Finally, they went to the shelter and picked that out."

"How did you live with a dog that vicious?"

I shrugged and said, "I just dealt with it. He usually didn't try to kill me when my parents were around. And if I was alone, I'd mostly just stay in my bedroom with the door closed, so it wasn't so bad."

"How long have your parents had that thing?"

"About twelve years." I swung a particularly heavy bag into the truck bed.

Dante stopped what he was doing and looked at me. "Your parents got that thing when you were a kid? And then they *kept it*, even after it started terrorizing their son?"

"Really? That surprises you? My parents threw out their only child and all of his stuff, just because I had the audacity to be honest with them and tell them I was gay." I swung another bag into the truck. "My mother loves that dog. No way was she getting rid of him."

"That's epically fucked up," Dante muttered.

"Welcome to my world."

When we were both seated in the cab of my pickup, Dante turned to me and said, "I don't know about you, but I'm starving. Want to grab something to go and take it back to your apartment? That way we can eat right after we haul your stuff inside."

"Good idea. Where should we go?"

"We're only a few blocks from Flannigan's. We could swing by there and pick up some of my grandmother's pasta with marinara."

"Nolan's," I corrected. "And what do you mean, your grandmother's pasta?"

"I put a dish on the menu when I owned that place, before Dmitri cheated at cards and won it from me," Dante said as I started the truck and rolled down the alley. His door swung open, and he cursed and slammed it shut a couple times.

"I'd forgotten that the bar was yours for a while. How long did you own it?"

"Just six months. It was a pain in the ass. The profit margin was too small for the number of hours it took to run the place properly. That's why I let Dmitri win it from me. I was glad to get rid of it."

I pulled up in the back alley behind Nolan's and parked illegally, and he took my hand as we went in the employee entrance. Dante greeted the cooks by name, and placed a to-go order through the pass-through window. He still acted like he owned the place.

He then swung me around and pinned me to the wall, and kissed me gently. He laced his fingers with mine and pulled my hands up and pinned them to the wall too, one on either side of my head.

"This is a lot of PDA," I murmured, feeling the color rise in my cheeks.

"You're already out at work. Everyone knows you're Jamie's ex," Dante said. "Besides, this isn't 'public' per se.

It's not like I'm sexually molesting you out in the dining room." He kissed me again, more deeply this time.

I noticed movement out of the corner of my eye and turned my head to look at Dmitri, who'd just come out of the office. He assessed the situation quickly with raised eyebrows, then smiled and said, "Hi guys. Don't tell me, let me guess. You're here for the spaghetti, aren't you, Dante?"

"Hi Dmitri," he said with a friendly grin. "Of course I am, and if you ever take it off the menu, I'm going to kick your ass." Embarrassingly enough, Dante kept me pinned to the wall during this little exchange, my hands still up beside my head.

"Good luck with that," Dmitri told him, but he said it affectionately. The two were old friends. He turned and went back through the door.

Not five seconds later, Jamie poked his head out of the office and stared at me. Apparently Dmitri had 'told on me' and Jamie had come to see it for himself. Dante was busy kissing my neck, so I knit my brows at my ex over the top of Dante's head and tried to will Jamie to go away.

Jamie mouthed the word, "Really?" He thought Dante was seriously bad news, so this wasn't sitting well with him. I rolled my eyes at him and said nothing. After a moment, Jamie frowned and ducked back into his office.

Cole was up next, coming to the pass-through to pick up an order. "Hey, you're back," he said to me. "Hi, Mr. Dombruso."

"Hi Cole," Dante replied, before kissing and nibbling my earlobe. As if this all wasn't embarrassing enough, my cock leapt to attention at the thing he was doing to my ear. Who knew those two body parts were hardwired together?

"You're still here," I said to Cole lightly, even as my face burned with a ferocious blush.

"Yeah. Well, you know, after earning a whopping fourteen dollars during the lunch shift, I gladly agreed to stay and work a second shift when Ruby called in sick." Cole leaned forward and tilted his head a couple inches to observe what Dante was doing to my ear. Then he looked at me and grinned. If embarrassment was lethal, someone would be making my funeral arrangements right about now. His food came up, and Cole grabbed a couple plates and headed back to the dining room with a cheerful, "Have fun, you two."

"Oh, we will," Dante said, grinning and looking into my eyes before going back to kissing me. Eventually one of the cooks came out of the kitchen carrying a big brown paper bag, which he handed to my date. Dante thanked him and gave him some cash, then took my hand and led me out the back door. Phase two of our date was under way.

Chapter Three

We cut through Golden Gate Park and double-parked in front of my apartment in the Sunset District. Dante and I worked as a team and got all the big, black garbage bags lined up against a wall of my living room in just a couple minutes. He volunteered to go and park my truck, and while he did that I unpacked our dinner, using an upended plastic milk crate as our table.

He came in through my open front door and closed and locked it behind him as he said, "I like what you've done here," indicating the milk crate with the two spaghetti dinners balanced on it. "Very Lady and the Tramp. But it's missing something." He sat down on the floor, reached into the pocket of his suit jacket and pulled out a sleek silver lighter, then jury-rigged it somehow so it would stay on. He slid the end of the lighter between the diamond-shaped weave of the milk crate so it was standing upright, then said, "There we go. Candlelight."

"Well, lighter light, technically, but it's cute. Do you smoke?"

"No."

"Then why do you carry a lighter?"

"Because sometimes," he said with a little smile, "you need a lighter."

"Like when you're recreating a scene from a Disney movie."

"Exactly." He picked up a bottle of red wine, which I'd been surprised to find included in the takeout bag, and said, "Do you have a corkscrew?"

"Uh, no. I don't even have a chair. Why would I have a corkscrew?"

He grinned and pulled out a little pocket knife, then folded out a tiny corkscrew.

"What else have you got in that jacket, MacGyver?"

"Wouldn't you like to know." He winked at me and worked the corkscrew expertly, and soon pulled the cork out with a flourish. "Should I even ask about glasses?"

"Nope."

He considered this for a beat, then said, "Alright," and took a sip directly from the bottle before passing it to me. "This has been a night of many firsts. I don't think I've ever drunk directly from a wine bottle before. Nor have I had a picnic on a milk crate."

"Nor have you hopped fences, picked locks, or faced down killer zombie lap dogs. It *has* been a night of many firsts for you. Makes me think you don't get out much," I teased. It felt surprisingly comfortable, hanging out with Dante and joking with him. More so than I'd ever have predicted when I first met him.

"Apparently I don't," he agreed. "This night, and you, have been wonderfully unexpected." He held my gaze, a slow, easy smile illuminating his handsome face.

"Here's to more nights like this one." I raised the wine bottle in a toast before taking a sip. Then I immediately erupted into a totally unflattering coughing fit, shielding my mouth with the crook of my elbow. In response, he offered me a clean handkerchief with a little grin. "Seriously?" I choked out, but as I said that, I took the handkerchief and used it to blot my watering eyes.

I loved the way his dark eyes sparkled when he found something funny. He asked, "So, how's the wine?"

"*So* gross. Gah. It's like drinking turpentine."

"You'd know this because you've drunk a lot of turpentine?"

"Uh, no. But I've *smelled* turpentine, and can easily imagine that it would taste exactly like that crap."

Dante smiled widely, then picked up the bottle and took a sip. When he put it down again, he said, "This is actually an excellent vintage."

"Ugh. Don't go all wine snob on me. That's so annoying." I was smiling though as I said that, and got up and went into the kitchen. I was back moments later with two cans of soda. "It's bad enough you showed up to go breaking and entering in a three thousand dollar suit. If you prove to be a wine snob on top of that, then there's just no hope for you."

"I'm curious. How exactly did you arrive at that dollar amount for this suit?" he asked as he slipped out of his jacket and set it on the floor beside him.

"I picked what I considered a totally unreasonable amount to spend on a suit, and then I doubled it. How far off am I?"

"You're fairly close," he said with an enigmatic smile as he unbuttoned his cuffs and rolled his sleeves back.

"Oh man. If you tell me my three thousand dollar estimate is actually too low, then I really can't hang out with you anymore," I told him with a smirk, and reached for a slice of garlic bread.

"Wait!" he exclaimed, and I froze in mid-reach. He got on his hands and knees and crawled around the crate to me, and then he kissed me, deeply, passionately, before sitting down beside me and handing me a piece of bread. He got one for himself, too.

It took me a minute to regain the power of speech, my heart pounding and electricity shooting through my body. I asked, once I'd calmed down a little, "To what do I owe that moment of passion?"

He smiled at me cheerfully and said, holding up his slice of bread, "We're both about to end up with truly offensive garlic breath. I have a theory that since we're both eating the same thing, it'll cancel itself out. But just in case I'm wrong, I wanted to do that before it became totally disagreeable to kiss me."

"Good thought."

As we ate our meal, Dante entertained me with tales of his bimonthly poker game. It included many prominent San Francisco business leaders, almost all of which, apparently, had to be watched like hawks because they were total cheaters. It was in that poker game that he'd won the bar from Bud Flannigan a few months back, and the same game in which Jamie's husband had gone on to win it from Dante.

When all the food was gone and Dante had polished off most of the bottle of wine, he pushed me onto my back on the floor and kissed me as he laid partially on top of me. A tremor of desire went through me even as part of my brain started to gear up in panic, just in case it turned out that we'd reached the wild monkey sex portion of the evening.

He said, "I think my theory about the garlic cancelling itself out because we both ate it has proven to be sound. What do you think?"

"I think you're right." I carefully unwound myself from his arms and got to my feet, stalling for time. "I'm going to get this cleaned up. Then I want to check those sacks we brought back from my parents' house. I want to make sure there aren't a few bags of actual garbage mixed in that might start attracting rodents," I said with a little shudder (because rodents are pretty much the grossest thing in the world). I grabbed the containers from our dinner and carried them through to the kitchen.

The pasta had come in heavy plastic containers, so I decided to wash them and keep them as dishes. Dante came into the room carrying some of the wrappers from our meal and deposited them in the trash. He raised an eyebrow when he saw me washing the containers, then opened a cupboard and took a peek inside. It was completely empty. "Ah," he said, answering his own unspoken question about what I was doing.

It took only a couple minutes to tidy up after dinner, and then I dried my hands on my jeans and went and took a look in a couple of the black garbage bags. The first two contained most of my wardrobe. When I opened the third bag, I went very still.

Dante noticed that immediately and crossed the room to me, gently touching my arm. "You okay, Charlie?"

"Yeah," I answered automatically.

"What's in that bag?"

It took me a minute to answer, and when I did I said softly, "My childhood."

Dante leaned over and tugged the bag open. Inside were all the framed photos of me as a child from my parents' house, and all the photo albums from when I was growing up. There were also stacks of report cards and school projects and drawings, mementos and keepsakes. I pulled a bent and wrinkled drawing out of the bag. It was one I'd done at about the age of six or seven, a crayon sketch of the house I'd grown up in, the house I'd broken into just a few hours ago, with bright flowers in the front yard and a cheerful yellow sun overhead. "They've completely gotten rid of me," I whispered.

I'd been trying so hard to be brave about all of this. To just deal with it. I kept trying to tell myself to be mad, not hurt, because somehow that seemed like a better response to what my parents had done to me. But I *was* hurt. More than that. I was devastated.

A few tears rolled down my cheeks, and I brushed them away with the back of my hand. Dante put an arm around my waist and handed me yet another clean, white, monogrammed handkerchief. I burst out laughing at that, but it sounded slightly hysterical. In the next moment, I was doubled over and sobbing. I dropped to my knees, wrapping myself into a little ball as wretched sobs shook my body. Dante knelt beside me wordlessly, wrapped his arms around me and rested his head on my back, holding me securely.

I don't know how long I cried. It could have been minutes or hours. I just let all of it out, all the hurt, the pain, the anger, as I completely gave myself over to my tears. I mourned the loss of my family, the loss of their love, the loss of the home I'd grown up in, the life I'd had. It had been so much to lose.

Finally my tears slowed, then stopped. I realized I was laying on the floor of my living room with Dante wrapped around me like a protective shell, pressed against my back. I rolled over in his arms and clung to him, and he held me tightly. He didn't say anything, he didn't offer advice, or try to reassure me that everything was going to be okay. He just held on to me, and it was so perfectly right.

When I trusted my voice to work, I whispered, "I'm sorry." It sounded raspy from all the crying.

"Angel, you have no reason to apologize."

"I do. I'm so sorry to put you through that. You were having fun. You were enjoying our date, and then I had to go and ruin it for you by—" I didn't get to finish my apology. Dante took hold of my chin and tilted it upward, so gently, and his lips found mine. The kiss was tender and sweet. It was more than that, too. It held so much promise.

We stayed on the floor, kissing for a long time. Then Dante sat up and leaned against the wall. He unfastened the top button of his shirt and loosened his tie, and pulled me onto his lap, wrapping his arms around me securely once again.

"We can't sit like this," I murmured, even as I snuggled against his shoulder. "I'm too heavy. Your legs will go numb."

He just went right on holding me as he murmured, "No they won't."

After a while I said randomly, "This was my first real first date. Jamie and I never dated. We just sort of transitioned over a long period of time from friends who hung out to friends who made out. Then when I broke up with him, I started going out with a girl named Callie."

"I didn't realize you're bisexual."

"I'm not. I was with Callie because I thought I could deny who and what I was. I thought I could force myself into a straight lifestyle. It got pretty serious between her and me, even though we never slept together. I even got as far as asking her to marry me, and she actually said yes. Our engagement didn't last long. I recently admitted to her that I was gay, and we broke up. She should hate my guts for doing that to her. I don't know why she doesn't."

"I think it would be impossible to hate you," Dante said quietly, running his hand over my hair.

"Oh, it's not impossible. She really should hate me now. I feel so bad for letting her get caught up in the lie I was trying to tell myself." After a pause I said, "I'm not sure why I started talking about that."

"You were telling me about your dating history."

"Oh, that's right. Yeah, I dated Callie for a few months, but that was just going through the motions as I tried to be something I wasn't. So when you think about it, this, tonight, was my first *real* date. We spent it breaking into my parents' house and then burning through your handkerchief collection as I totally had an emotional breakdown on my living room floor." I sighed and said, "I was wrong to pull you into my fucked up family drama. I don't know what I was thinking, bringing you along. Except that I really didn't want to do this alone, and I didn't know who else to ask, and then you came to the bar, and—"

"I'm so glad you didn't do that alone."

"You must be so damn sorry you ever asked me out," I said with a sad little smile, my head still on his shoulder.

"On the contrary. This has been one of the best nights of my life."

I chuckled a little at that. "If there was any possible way that was true, I'd really worry about what the rest of your life must be like."

"It's absolutely true." I sat up a bit to look at him as he said, "I don't date. It's just not something I do. The last time I even attempted it was with Dmitri, and that was over two years ago. I'm lucky that fiasco didn't end up costing me a friendship."

"So, if you don't date, what do you do?"

"I fuck."

"Ah."

"You won't believe me when I tell you I'm so glad we had this night, instead of the one I had planned. I was just going to buy you dinner, then take you straight to bed."

"Oh, I can easily believe that you wouldn't want to sleep with me after this."

"That's in no way what I just said. I'm saying I'm glad I got to spend time with you, talking to you, laughing and crying with you, getting to know you. I still fully intend to take you to bed in the near future, provided you'll consent to going out with me again. And while I wholeheartedly look forward to that, I'm grateful that we got to do this, too."

"You'd have to be insane to actually ask me out again."

"Charlie, will you please go out with me tomorrow night?"

"Okay." I held him a little tighter and kissed his shoulder. "It really is nuts, you know, wanting to go out with me again after what I just subjected you to."

"It's crazy that you agreed to go out with me in the first place."

"Oh yeah, saying yes to an incredibly hot, sexy, fascinating man, clearly that's completely crazy."

"But you must have known who I am, what I do," he said quietly. "Or if you didn't, you obviously found out soon after I asked you out. But you still gave me a second chance and agreed to go out with me tonight."

"I'm so glad I did."

His dark eyes searched my face. "Don't you want to know who you're getting mixed up with? Don't you have questions about my line of work?"

"You know, when I first agreed to go out with you, I was also thinking this was only going to be about sex. You'd fuck me, and that would be it. What you did didn't really matter to me, because you were just going to be a fling. Now I feel like I *do* know who I'm getting mixed up with, because you showed me who you really are tonight." He pulled me to him and kissed me gently.

We kissed for a long time, sweet and tender giving way to hot and heavy. I ended up straddling Dante's lap, my hard cock pressed against his through our clothes. He pulled my t-shirt off and ran his hands over my body, and then he swung me onto my back on the living room floor and stripped me, so that I was completely naked while he remained clothed. I laughed self-consciously when I realized that, and he rolled over and pulled me on top of him, his hands sliding down my back to cup my ass. He rocked me gently, rubbing me against his cock as we kissed.

Dante surprised me by rolling me onto my back on the floor again, sliding down my body and taking my cock down his throat. I was already so aroused that I just went with it, pushing down the panic that usually accompanied sex and focusing on the incredible pleasure Dante was sending through me. I propped myself up on my elbows and watched him, his dark head moving up and down between my legs. And then he looked up at me.

The moment we made eye contact was electric. I think I actually gasped. But who knows, because I was panting and moaning, totally caught up in the moment, totally caught up in Dante. He held my gaze as he brought me right up to orgasm, and then swallowed me to the root and took me right over the edge. I cried out, throwing my head back and bucking my hips as his warm, wet mouth kept working me. He sucked me until I was totally drained and I collapsed back on the floor, sweaty and shaking, trying to catch my breath.

Finally, he slid his mouth off my cock and sat up, leaning against the wall. Again he pulled me onto his lap, cradling me securely. As I held on to him, my body still shaking a bit as I came down off that incredibly intense orgasm, he said, "Thank you."

"What are you thanking me for?" I asked. His black hair was a little long, and I brushed it back from his eyes as I met his gaze.

"For letting me do that to you."

"I think you have that backwards," I said with a big grin. "I'm the one who should be doing the thanking." I kissed him before asking, "Would you like me to do that for you now?"

"Not tonight, Charlie. I just wanted to make you feel good. I don't want anything in return, apart from this." He hugged me to him and kissed me gently.

After a while, he slid me off his lap and stood up, then took my hand and pulled me to my feet as he said, "Come on, angel. It's late, let's get you to bed."

"Will you spend the night with me?"

"I'm sorry, I can't," he said, and I felt a stab of disappointment. "I just can't sleep in unfamiliar places. But I'll get you tucked in before I take off."

"K," I murmured, and let him lead me to the bedroom.

He pushed the door open and stopped short when he flipped on the overhead light. The room was empty except for a cheap air mattress topped with a thin pillow and thinner blanket, my gym bag open on the floor beside it. Dante frowned and asked, "When is your furniture supposed to arrive?"

I grinned at that. "Well, whenever my neighbors decide they don't want some of their stuff anymore and drag it out to the curb for disposal. Shortly after that, it will 'arrive' in my apartment, after I drag it up the stairs."

"You haven't bought yourself anything? Not even a bed?"

"I made nine dollars today by working the nonexistent lunch rush," I told him. "So for now, it's air mattresses and milk crates with a forecast for secondhand castoffs, hopefully in the near future."

"You can't live like this," Dante said, knitting his brows. "Get dressed. You can stay in my guest room until we get your apartment squared away."

I crossed the room to the air mattress and slid under the blanket. "This is fine."

"This room is really depressing," Dante told me. "You're not spending the night here."

"Sure I am."

"Please come home with me."

"I appreciate your concern, Dante, but I'm happy here. If Jamie wasn't making me a great deal on this sublet, I'd be living in my truck right now. So to me, this place isn't depressing. It's a palace."

Dante considered that for a long moment. Then he turned off the overhead light and crossed the room to me. I could see him pretty clearly in the illumination provided by the streetlight outside my bare window. He sunk down carefully on a corner of the air mattress and said, "What are the chances this thing can hold both of us without exploding?"

"Slim to none. But let's live dangerously." I stretched out on my side, and he pulled off his tie and his shoes and lay down gingerly beside me, gathering me into his arms. I ran my palms up his broad back and snuggled against him as I murmured, "What are you doing? I thought you were going to deposit me in my bed and be done with me for tonight."

"I *was* going to deposit you in your bed, back when I thought you *had* a bed."

"And now, what? You're staying to compensate for the lack of furniture?"

His laugh was deep, warm and genuine. "I'm staying because you're too stubborn to come with me when I tell you to."

I said, "You didn't want to spend the night with me. There's no reason for you to stay."

"Are you telling me to leave?"

"Well, no."

"Okay then." He shifted a bit, settling in. "Just so you know, I'm going to go home sometime during the night. I'll never be able to sleep here. But I'll stay long enough for you to fall asleep."

"You never really explained why you're even staying that long," I murmured drowsily as I cuddled against him.

"I just can't walk away and leave you all alone in this depressing room with this depressing air mattress." And after a few moments, he said quietly, "I'm staying because you make me want to protect you like I've never wanted to protect anyone or anything in my life."

I mulled that over as I nestled into the space between his chin and shoulder. And then I whispered, "Thank you."

Chapter Four

It was disappointing to wake up alone the next morning, even though Dante had forewarned me, and not entirely surprising to find myself lying on the hard floor. The cheap air mattress had indeed not been up to the task of holding both of us last night. But instead of exploding, it had apparently slowly and anticlimactically leaked to death.

I got up off the floor and padded into the kitchen, in search of my morning caffeine. It was going to have to take the form of a can of soda, because that was all I had here.

Or it *used to be* all I had here. I stopped short at the sight of a shiny new coffee maker on my counter, coffee pot full, a couple white mugs lined up beside it. There was a pink bakery box on the counter, too, and I flipped the lid to find an assortment of bagels. A search of the kitchen revealed Dante had also bought me groceries, pots and pans, silverware and dishes. Really? Where did someone even *find* dishes this early in the morning?

Wow, talk about over the top.

Sweet, though.

But definitely over the top.

I had some coffee while standing at my kitchen counter, then went into the bathroom and found a note taped to my mirror with a bandage (not like I had any actual tape). It said:

Good morning, angel. I hope you slept well. Please text me when you get up. D.

After using the restroom, I located my phone and sent the following text to Dante: *The kitchen transformation was quite a surprise. You really shouldn't have, but thank you.*

Within a minute he replied: *You're welcome. Are you dressed?*

Okay, that was odd. I texted, *No.*

Get dressed, angel, he wrote.

I started to ask why, but then I really didn't want to be hanging around naked anyway. I grabbed a pair of gym shorts out of my duffle bag and pulled them on, then dropped the phone into my pocket. About a minute later, there was a knock at the door.

A burly guy with a clipboard was standing in the hall. He looked at me disinterestedly and asked, "Charlie Connolly?"

"Yes."

"Delivery."

"I didn't order anything," I told him.

"I know."

I raised my brows at him. "Does this have something to do with Dante Dombruso?"

"Yes, sir."

Oh my God, seriously? "Well, please take it back. Whatever it is, please tell Dante I said thanks, but no thanks."

The kitchen items were already too much. Whatever now required a burly deliveryman was *certainly* too much.

"That's not an option, sir."

"I'm sorry?"

A second big burly guy appeared beside the first and asked, "Do we have a problem here?"

"The kid wants us to take the stuff back," Burly Guy Number One told him.

"That's not an option," Burly Guy Number Two said.

I rolled my eyes at that. "So if I close and lock this door, what do you think you're going to do? Knock it down and force me to take whatever over the top thing Dombruso decided to send me? What is it, anyway?"

The guy with the clipboard flipped to a second sheet of paper and recited, "California king mattress, box spring and bed frame. Dining table. Two chairs. Bedroom set. Two boxes of miscellaneous items."

I stared at the men outside my door. Once I'd scraped my jaw up off the floor, I pulled the phone from my pocket, typed *Seriously?* and hit send.

A few seconds later, Dante replied, *Just take the gifts, Charlie.*

I wrote: *The kitchen items were already too much. This is way, way, way too much!*

I want you to have these things, Charlie. Please don't argue.

I don't feel right about accepting them.

Please, Charlie. Take the gifts. For me.

That weakened my resolve. *I don't feel comfortable with this, Dante.*

I know, angel, but this means a lot to me. I want to do this for you. Please let me.

If he had insisted I take them, I would have refused. But this gentle approach wore me down. I chewed my lip for a while, then sighed and stepped aside for the deliverymen.

I went into the kitchen to get out of their way, and sat on the counter. I started composing a message to Dante about how, though I appreciated the thought, he really shouldn't do things like this. It was long and rambling and sounded really ungrateful. I deleted the message without sending it, and sent this one instead: *Thank you.*

He wrote back: *Thank you for making me so happy, angel.*

That made me feel good. I wrote: *Please let this be the last of it, Dante. I can't keep taking from you like this.*

He replied: *The living room set I wanted for you is on backorder and will be arriving later in the week. But after that I'll stop. Probably.*

I sighed at that and wrote: *Where does someone even buy a king-size mattress before nine a.m. on a Tuesday morning?*

I own a furniture store, among other things, so that was easy.

How convenient. *Thank you again, Dante. This was really nice of you. Totally and completely over the top, but nice of you. I will of course repay you for every cent of it, even if it takes me the next ten years.*

The only repayment I'll accept, he wrote, *will be the sight of your smiling face enjoying your new things.*

One of the deliverymen carried a little round table into the room and set it up in the breakfast nook at the back of the kitchen. It had a black wrought iron frame and a glass top that overlaid a beautiful stone mosaic surface. He left the room and came back with two wrought iron chairs, each with a thick sand-colored cushion. The set was obviously finely made, both functional and artistic. Not that I knew a damn thing about design, but if I had to guess, I'd say it looked like something you'd find in a little courtyard in Italy.

I smiled at that. Dante Dombruso seemed like the kind of man who did everything intentionally. So, this seemed like a way of asserting a little of his Italian-American self into my home. I really didn't mind that. On the contrary, I liked having a bit of Dante around.

When I was again alone in the kitchen, I went and sat at the little table and ran a fingertip over the cool glass surface, tracing the tidy, regular pattern of small brown and gold and sand-colored pebbles beneath the glass.

A few minutes later, Delivery Guy Number One stuck his head into the kitchen. "We're all done here. We'll be back later in the week, just as soon as your living room furniture arrives in the warehouse."

"Thank you," I said and followed him to the front door, closing and locking it behind him. I then went and took a look at the bedroom.

The bed was absolutely enormous. It took up most of the room, and was made up with new sheets, blankets and several pillows in tranquil shades of green and blue. It all nestled in a big, black, wrought iron bed frame that looked expensive and elegant and really, really heavy. I wondered what I'd possibly do with that when Jamie's lease was up in a few months and I had to move into a cheaper apartment.

I wondered what I was going to do with *any* of it when I had to move. In addition to the massive bed, the room now also contained a dark wood dresser and a matching set of night stands, topped with attractive lamps. Missing from the room was the flat air mattress.

I went and checked the closet. My thin blanket was folded up on the shelf with the flat pillow on top of it. The gym bag was in there on the floor, and a nice new set of wooden clothes hangers lined the dowel. Now that was attention to detail.

The workers had stopped short of hanging my things up, thank goodness. I pulled my clothes out of the bag and put them on hangers, and stuck my socks and underwear in the top drawer of the dresser. I'd tackle the garbage bags with the rest of my clothes later. For now I climbed up on the bed, stretched out on top of the thick comforter and stared at the ceiling.

Talk about mixed emotions. On one hand, I was incredibly grateful to Dante, and so happy to have a comfortable bed. But on the other hand, I felt guilty about accepting this stuff. It was just too much. It didn't feel right, him spending this kind of money on me.

Never mind the fact that he just met me. Obviously I'd made quite an impression on him on our first date. And apparently, the impression was that I was a pathetic kid that needed lots and lots of care.

I pulled my phone from my pocket and drummed my fingers on the plastic case for a moment, then typed: *Thank you again, Dante. The deliverymen just left. Everything is incredibly beautiful. It reminds me of you.*

He soon replied: *I'm so glad you like it, and thank you for the compliment.*

Maybe I should have just been gracious and left it at that. But instead I wrote: *Am struggling a bit to come to grips with all of this. Wish you were here with me. Would feel better if we could talk about it.*

The phone rang in my hand, and I answered it with a soft, "Hi."

"Hi angel." Dante had a rich, deep voice that I found incredibly soothing. I closed my eyes and let the sound of it wash over me. "You doing alright?"

"I'm overwhelmed," I told him honestly. "It's just so much, Dante. No one's ever done anything like this for me."

"I know it must seem over the top, but please just enjoy it, Charlie. Like I said, I own a furniture store, so it was really easy to do this for you and it gave me so much pleasure."

"That part I like," I said quietly. "Giving you pleasure, I mean."

"Same here, angel. I wanted to do this for you to make you feel good. I want you to be happy."

"Thank you, Dante. I appreciate it so much. I do. But it also…it also makes me feel guilty," I admitted, and curled up on my side.

"Why would it make you feel guilty?"

Someone knocked on the door, and I sighed and ignored it. "I don't know. I just do. I feel like I don't deserve it."

"Aren't you going to get the door?" Dante asked.

"No. It's probably just someone selling something."

"Get the door, Charlie," he said gently.

I sighed and did as I was told, bringing the phone with me as I left the bedroom and said, "Okay. Hang on, please. I'll only be a minute."

I swung open the door to find Dante standing there, phone in hand, concerned expression on his handsome face. I pulled the phone from my ear and stammered, "What are you doing here?"

"Your text said 'wish you were here with me.' So here I am."

"You dropped everything and ran right over? Why?" I stepped back and held the door open for him, staring at him in amazement.

"Why? Because you wanted to talk to me," Dante said, and drew me into his arms. "Fortunately, I happened to be close by."

That was absolutely astonishing to me, the fact that I mattered enough to him to come right over because of an offhand comment. "Thank you," I whispered, clinging to him for just a moment before releasing him and stepping back embarrassedly.

He put his phone in the pocket of his black wool overcoat, then took my hand and led me to the bedroom. Dante looked appraisingly at the new furniture as he said, "Come sit down and talk to me, Charlie. We'll have to do that in here because your living room furniture has yet to arrive."

I let him lead me to the bed and sat beside him on the plush mattress, drawing one of the pillows onto my lap. The one I'd grabbed was pale green on one side, deep blue on the other, the fabric slightly iridescent. I ran my hand over it absently. It was smooth, cool, and silky to the touch. "I knew that'd be the perfect color combination," he murmured. When

I glanced at him, he said, "When I picked out the linens, I was imagining you lying naked in this bed, your gorgeous skin offset against the deep blue sheets. I also thought of the extraordinary pale jade green of your eyes, and just knew these colors would be right for you."

I slid close and put my arms around him and kissed him, and he pulled me to him and deepened the kiss. That reminded me of something, and I stood up abruptly, stammering, "Hang on a minute, okay? I'll be right back." I fled to the bathroom.

I brushed my teeth quickly, then ran a comb over my hair, which was sticking up in every direction. I wished I wasn't dressed in ratty gym shorts left over from high school, but oh well.

He was right where I left him, perched on the edge of the bed, watching me closely when I came out of the bathroom. I was beginning to realize that was a thing with him, the careful scrutiny. There was a sharp intelligence in his dark eyes, he was clearly a man who missed nothing. He was serious and focused at the moment, a different version of himself than the relaxed, playful Dante who'd broken into my parents' house with me. I could tell he was concerned that his gesture of kindness was going to backfire and make me upset with him.

I sat down beside him and picked up his hand with both of mine. "Thank you again for the furniture. I really do appreciate it, so much. I'm sorry I was acting weird about it." I raised his hand to my lips and kissed it.

He looked into my eyes and said, "Please never, ever think you don't deserve good things, Charlie. You deserve them more than anyone I've ever met." He kissed me again before drawing me into his arms and holding me securely.

I whispered very quietly, "Thank you for taking care of me."

*****

When I arrived at work a couple hours later for the super exciting lunch shift, my thoughts were still on Dante. He'd stayed for only a few minutes that morning, just long enough to kiss me and reassure me and make me feel so incredibly happy. Then he had to leave for a day of meetings (about what I couldn't begin to guess).

I was sort of daydreaming, my work shirt in my hands, when Jamie stuck his head in the employee dressing room and said, "Hey Charlie. Could you come and see me in my office before you begin your shift?"

I nodded, then frowned at his retreating back. Okay, first of all, being called into your ex-boyfriend's office like he was the principal and you were a naughty school kid was sort of degrading. Secondly, I knew what that little discussion was going to be about, and boy, did I *not* want to hear Jamie's opinions on my love life.

I got dressed for my shift, then stuck a neutral expression on my face and went to his office. "Hi," I said from the doorway. "Where's Dmitri?" I almost never saw one of them without the other.

"He had to run over to his sister Ani's apartment, but he'll be here soon. Sit down, Charlie."

I sank onto one of the wooden chairs in front of his desk, and took a good, long look at my ex for the first time in days. He was growing his hair out now that he no longer worked in law enforcement. The light brown was streaked with golden blond and always looked a bit tousled. He was surfing much more frequently these days, so his tan was deeper, bringing out his blue eyes. All of those things made him look like he had in high school. Like he had when I first fell in love with him. I dropped my gaze to my hands, which were folded in my lap.

"I'm worried about you, Charlie."

"You don't need to worry about me. I'm fine," I said, still not making eye contact.

"It scares me that you're getting mixed up with Dante Dombruso," he said, cutting right to the chase. "The man's dangerous. I mean really, really dangerous. In all likelihood, he's a killer, and the list of illegal activities he's involved in is longer than my arm."

"He won't hurt me," I said quietly.

"You say that based on what?"

I shrugged and said, "I feel good around him. Safe. I'm trusting my instincts, and they're telling me Dante is okay."

He wrinkled his brow in concern and said, "I care about you, Charlie. You're like, the most innocent guy on the planet, and I hate the thought of this guy taking advantage of you."

"You don't know him."

"And you do?"

"I'm getting to know him, and he's been absolutely wonderful so far." I grinned as I thought about his sweet concern that morning, rushing over because I said I wished we could talk and then holding me and kissing me and making me feel so good.

"Oh man. You're totally falling for him."

"What if I am?" *Was I?*

"I just want you to be careful, especially if you decide to sleep with him."

"Wow. Okay, thank you for the sex talk, Jamie. I didn't realize you'd stepped into the role of my dad after my real one disowned me," I said, crossing my arms over my chest.

"Oh, don't get all sarcastic and defensive, Charlie. I'm just trying to help. I can't sit back and watch you headed for disaster. You know I can't."

"I appreciate your concern, but there's no reason to be worried about this."

"Really." Jamie looked totally unconvinced.

"I need to go help Cole set up, because your bar opens in ten minutes. Are you done with your lecture?" I asked.

"That wasn't a lecture."

"It was a *little bit* of a lecture."

"It was a friend expressing concern."

"In the form of a lecture."

"Fine. I'm done lecturing, even though it wasn't a lecture. Just…be careful, Charlie."

"Message received, loud and clear. I'm totally going to ignore it, just so you know. But it was received." I got up from my chair and started to leave, then impulsively turned back to Jamie and said, "Hey, could you do me a favor?"

"Of course. What is it?"

"Could you never summon me into your office again? It makes me feel like I'm back in high school and Principal Brewer is getting ready to chew my ass off. It's not a good feeling."

"Sorry. It was just a more private place to talk. I didn't mean to induce a principal's office flashback."

"I know," I said before heading out the door.

I'd expected yet another lunch shift so deserted that tumbleweeds would be rolling through the dining room, but we actually had a couple customers. When a four-top was

73

seated in my section, I was excited until I saw who it was. Then I felt like crawling under a rock.

The four women in the booth were people I knew all too well. I pressed my eyes shut for a long moment, then made myself stick a smile on my face and walk up to them with a cheerful, "Hi ladies. How's it going?"

Jamie's best friend Jess greeted me with a smile and a friendly, "Hey, Charlie." Jamie and Jess had been inseparable since the first day of Kindergarten. When I was fifteen and transferred to their high school (for the better football program), they both took me under their wings.

Jess had been a great friend to me, before I'd been stupid enough to dump her best friend. She was still cordial to me after that, but we really weren't friends anymore. I didn't know why she was even cordial, actually. Jess was a cute, tiny badass, and I'd expected her to kick my butt after dumping Jamie the way I had.

I was also greeted with a smile by Callie McLoughlin. Now there was another woman who should, by all rights, want to beat the shit out of me. After our short engagement, which ended when I admitted to her that I was living a lie, gay, and in love with Jamie, she'd actually forgiven me and said she wanted to remain friends. God knows why.

Callie's two besties, Tina and Gina, who were seated in the booth with her and Jess, didn't share Callie's forgiving attitude, however. They thought I was the Devil incarnate, and were glaring at me like I was something disgusting they'd found stuck to the bottom of their stilettos.

"Hey Charlie. I'd heard you were working here," Callie said, still smiling. She had thick auburn hair that framed her face in soft waves, and freckles and big brown eyes. She was sweet and pretty and a really nice person, and had always been way too good for me. "How do you like it?"

I shrugged and said lightly, "It's good. The lunch shift has been pretty slow. But hey, beats the bug business." For a few months, at the same time that I was dating Callie and thought I could force myself to be straight, I'd made the incredibly stupid decision to go to work for my Uncle Al's exterminator business. It was all part of some grand, totally misguided plan to grow up and be responsible: wife, family business, eventually a house and kids, the whole stereotypical nine yards. I'd been such an idiot.

"Yeah, no doubt. So hey, want to have lunch some time?" she asked. "I'd really like to catch up." Callie was taking the let's-be-friends thing seriously.

"I'd like that. Text me with a time and place and I'll be there. So," I said, looking around the table, "what can I bring everyone to drink?" At least Tina and Gina would get to boss me around for an hour or so, which ought to be fun for them. I repressed a sigh.

Callie and her group lingered for a couple hours. Jamie and Dmitri pulled up chairs and joined them at some point, drinks and lunch and more drinks leaving all of them in a jovial mood. Their laughter and loud, happy conversation filled the dining room.

I'd known most of those people for years. Some of them even used to love me, either as a friend, or as much more than that. But I felt like such an outsider as I waited on them.

I totally knew it was me who'd damaged all these relationships. Me who'd royally fucked up. But knowing that didn't make it hurt any less.

It was beginning to seem like this lunch shift was never going to end, that Callie and company were never going to leave, that Jamie and Dmitri were never going to go back to work. But I was granted a brief reprieve when Cole asked me if I wanted to take a break and offered to watch my tables. I retreated to the most private place I could think of, the storage room. I sat against the wall, hugged my knees to my chest and sort of curled into myself, making myself as small as possible. I only had a few minutes for my break, and I really needed to get myself together, psych myself up so I'd be able to go back out there and stick a smile on my face and endure waiting on my former friends.

I was in there for probably sixty seconds before the door to the storage room opened and closed, and someone sat down right beside me. I didn't have to look up to see who it was. I recognized his cologne.

"Really?" I muttered, not raising my head from my knees.

"Why don't you join us, Charlie?" Dmitri said. "I know you must feel left out. Jamie's already asked you twice to pull up a chair. Why don't you take him up on it?"

I sighed and sat up, resting my head against the wall behind me, and took a look at Jamie's husband. Dmitri was a stunningly beautiful man. He had perfect, luminous skin, and perfect jet black hair, and perfect clothes, and like, two percent body fat. Instead of answering his questions, I said, "I want so much to hate you."

He smiled at that, revealing perfect teeth and a perfect set of perfect dimples. "No doubt," he said. "So, how's that going?"

"I'm failing at it, and I don't really know why. Sheer jealousy alone should have made it incredibly easy to hate you."

"Same here. I'm jealous of the history you two share, and I want to hate you for the way you dumped Jamie and hurt him. But, if you'd never done that, I wouldn't have met the love of my life. So instead, I find myself kind of grateful to you."

I grinned a little. "This is the first time you and I have ever had a one-on-one conversation," I said, "and we're talking about how much we wish we could hate each other. That's kind of bizarre, I suppose."

"Well, hey, at least we're talking." Dmitri was studying me closely, tilting his head to the side like a puppy. "Is it because I'm with them? Is that why you don't want to join your friends? If you want some time with them without me making you feel uncomfortable, I can go find something to do."

"They're not my friends anymore."

"Really? I guess someone forgot to tell them that," Dmitri said.

"Tina and Gina want to use me as a human speed bump."

"Okay, maybe. But everyone else at that table would love it if you joined us."

"Apart from you."

"No, including me. I want us to get to know each other, Charlie. Not only because we're working together, but because you're always going to be a part of Jamie's life. I really want you and me to be okay with one another."

"I'm not a part of Jamie's life. As much as I want to be friends with him, I know how badly I fucked up our friendship. It's damaged beyond repair."

"You're wrong. He still cares about you, and always will."

I said, "He feels sorry for me. That's it. Jamie's way too nice a guy to let me reach my full potential as a homeless, unemployed loser. Let's face it, without his intervention, that's exactly what I'd be right now."

"No you wouldn't. You'd have landed on your feet."

"You don't know me very well. When I fail at things, I fail epically."

"You know what this conversation needs?" Dmitri asked. He and I both said in unison, "Alcohol."

He got up and brushed off the seat of his dark jeans, then perused the shelves for a moment. "I'd suggest vodka, but I don't like it warm," he said. He grabbed another bottle off the shelf and held it up for me to see. "Tequila?"

"Why not?"

He removed the lid and offered the bottle to me first, and I took a long drink. I then immediately erupted into a massive coughing fit. I happened to have one of Dante's monogrammed handkerchiefs in my pocket, and I pulled it out and dabbed my tearing eyes as I handed the booze to Dmitri. He sat back down beside me and took the bottle as he said, "Oh my God, that's hilarious."

"What is?"

"The fact that you and I have so much in common."

"So you're also about to embarrass yourself with an alcohol-induced coughing fit?"

"No. Well, probably. But I meant that when I was going out with Dante, I somehow always ended up with a hankie of his in my pocket. I still don't know how so many of them found their way into my possession. To this day, I still find one occasionally among my things."

"It's probably because you never wanted to embarrass yourself by handing them back to him once you'd used them."

"Probably." Dmitri tipped back the bottle and took a long drink, and then a moment later had a coughing fit even more embarrassing than mine had been. I grinned and handed him Dante's handkerchief.

"I'm so glad you just did that," I told him with a big smile, once he'd stopped coughing and was blotting his eyes with the square of fabric.

He laughed at that. "Thanks."

"It's just such a pain in the ass, being around that much perfect," I grinned, gesturing at Dmitri by drawing a circle in the air around him with both of my hands. "It's nice to see you're actually human."

"Very human. And *very* far from perfect. Let's see if I can do better this time," he said, and took a cautious sip from the bottle. "It's better if you don't chug it."

He held out the tequila, and I took it and tried a couple cautious sips. "You're right. I was trying to look manly in front of you, that's why I went for the chug earlier. I should have known better than to try to pull off that kind of bullshit macho posturing."

Dmitri chuckled and said, "You're a very candid person, Charlie. I like that about you."

"Can I ask you something?"

"Sure."

"Why didn't it work out between you and Dante?"

He considered the question for a moment, leaning back against the wall behind him and adjusting the rolled back cuff of his dark blue button-down shirt. "I really like Dante, I always have. But mainly, we just didn't click as lovers."

"So, you and he slept together." I didn't know why that bothered me so much.

"Actually, no. We fooled around a bit, but we never actually fucked. He only tops, and I wasn't about to bottom with Dante. I knew better than to give up control with him." Dmitri grinned at me and said, "That's probably totally TMI. Sorry if I just over-shared." He'd already been drinking a lot with lunch, and apparently the tequila was working its magic on him as well.

"What do you mean about giving up control?"

"Well, you know. I knew it was a mistake, letting him feel he was in charge. He's the kind of man who'll totally take over your life if you let him. His control issues were something I wanted to steer clear of."

"He has control issues?"

"Big time. Haven't you noticed?"

"I don't know. Maybe a bit. He definitely, um, takes the lead when we do anything physical. But actually…I like that," I admitted embarrassedly. I took another drink of tequila while considering Dmitri's question, then said, "He did buy me a ton of furniture without asking first. Is that a control thing?"

Dmitri grinned and said, "Probably." I handed the bottle back to him and he drank some more before saying, "I hope you can look past the control issues, because I think you two could be really good together. I actually hope you end up with Dante long-term. Jamie wholeheartedly disagrees, because he only sees the line of work Dante's in. He doesn't see the man behind it."

"Is it bad? The stuff Dante's involved in?" I felt like a jerk for asking that, like I was going behind Dante's back or something, but I really wanted Dmitri's take on it.

He thought about that for a long moment, turning the tequila bottle around in his hands. Finally, he said, "Jamie would say yes unequivocally. But...well, you know I was raised in the Russian mafia. So, my take on Dante's line of work is going to be much different than the average person's. I understand the position Dante's in. He feels a sense of duty to his family. He does what he believes he has to. Yes, what he's involved in is illegal. Most people think if you're a criminal, you automatically must be a rotten person. But Dante's really not. I honestly believe he's an honorable man."

"An honorable criminal."

"Yeah."

"Ok." I said. "I can't quite grasp that, but I already know there's so much good in Dante. He's so sweet, and kind, and fun—"

"Fun?"

"Yeah. He's really fun."

"Dante Dombruso," Dmitri said incredulously. "Fun? I mean, don't get me wrong, I really like him. He's a good friend. But that has got to be the very last word I would ever apply to him."

I smiled broadly. "You should have seen him last night. I took him along to break into my parents' house to get some of my stuff out. It was pretty much a total fiasco, and he was so good-humored throughout all of it. He climbed over fences, and teased me about my Hello Kitty lock picking kit, and made comments about my parents' zombie lap dog. He was *fun*."

"Wow. You obviously bring out a side of him I've never seen, and I've known Dante for years. Wait, did you just say you have a Hello Kitty lock picking kit?" I nodded and he burst out laughing. Then I was laughing, too. A really unflattering snort burst from him, and we laughed even harder.

"Damn, I'm missing one hell of a good party." We both looked up at Jamie, who was leaning against the doorframe to the store room with a huge smile on his face. "I was wondering what had happened to both of you," he said. "My money was on fist fighting in the alley, but instead, I find you bonding over tequila. I'm so happy."

I got up off the floor and held my hand out to Dmitri, then hauled him to his feet. "Hi Jamie. You've always had really good taste in men," I told him with a big grin, which was totally the tequila talking. "You know, I wanted to hate Dmitri, but I just can't. In fact, I really like him, especially after that totally unflattering snort he just committed. That was hilarious. FYI, I think I'm a little drunk, and Dmitri definitely is. It's totally his fault, so don't fire me."

"Yup. Definitely missed one hell of a good party," Jamie said with a smile as he followed us out of the store room.

"Do I even want to ask about the zombie lap dog?" Dmitri asked as we headed back to the dining room. He was still chuckling.

"You really don't," I told him.

*****

I managed to sober up over the next hour. No more customers came in for lunch, and Cole continued to wait on Callie and company for me, so I didn't have to keep feeling like a reject. I busied myself with side work in the back, because even after Dmitri's and my bonding session, I still didn't feel comfortable joining their group.

As her friends finally headed for the door, Callie came and found me back by the kitchen. "Here, Charlie," she said, picking up my hand and turning it palm up. "I want to give this back." She set a little black jeweler's box in my hand and folded my fingers over it.

"No. No way," I told her. "We talked about this. The ring is yours, I want you to have it." I took her hand just like she'd done with mine and put the box in her palm, then sandwiched it gently between both of mine.

"It's not right for me to keep it, Charlie. You used all your savings on it. You should get your money back."

I shook my head. "It's yours. I get why you wouldn't want to wear it, but why don't you sell it and put the money toward that Mini Cooper you had your eye on? Or, you know, take a vacation or something. Whatever you want."

"I can't do that."

"Sure you can."

"Just take the ring, Charlie."

"Not happening."

I let go of her hands, and she sighed and tapped the box against her palm, regarding me for a long moment. "You're so stubborn, Charlie Connolly."

I smiled at her fondly. "No more than you, Callie McLoughlin."

She grinned and shook her head. "This discussion isn't over. I'll see you in a few days when we have lunch, and then

I'm getting you to take this ring back." She dropped the box into her purse.

I smiled and said, "Good luck with that," and then I impulsively leaned over and kissed her cheek. "I'll see you soon, Callie."

"Bye, Charlie." She gave me a look that was just the tiniest bit wistful, and then turned and left without looking back.

I sure as hell wasn't taking that engagement ring back, not now, not ever. That ring meant she'd left the relationship with *something* at least. No, it wouldn't absolve me of my guilt. It wouldn't in any way, shape or form make what I did to her okay. But I wanted her to use the money from its sale for something that would make her happy. I owed her that.

I sighed and got back to work.

Chapter Five

Dante picked me up for our date at five sharp. He was dressed in a black t-shirt, black cashmere sweater, and dark indigo jeans. It actually seemed odd to see him in something other than a suit, and I pointed this out to him.

He grinned and said, "The suit makes me look older, which is normally the whole point of wearing it. But around *some* people, it gives them the impression that I'm practically geriatric and on the verge of breaking a hip at any moment. So, I thought it would behoove me to dress down a bit."

"If you want to remind *some* people that you are, in fact, still in your twenties, you might also consider dropping words like *behoove* from your vocabulary. Just saying," I teased as I locked up my apartment and he took my hand. Okay, more PDA, but I could handle it. I was slowly adjusting to being out.

We reached his black BMW, which was double-parked in the street, and as he held the door open for me I asked, "Hey, how's your grandmother?"

"She's doing a lot better, thank you for asking. I just came from seeing her, actually. The doctors want to keep her in the hospital for another week, just to be on the safe side, which they'll regret. The entire nursing staff will probably flee the hospital and they'll face grave staffing shortages. My grandmother is kind of a terror." He smiled fondly.

"So where are we going?" I asked as he slid behind the wheel and put the key in the ignition.

"It's a surprise."

As soon as he pulled onto the southbound 101 freeway, I exclaimed, "We're going to Candlestick Park!"

"Now how the hell did you guess that so quickly?"

"There's no other reason to go this direction."

"There are a *million* other reasons to go this direction!"

"Not if you're me." I leaned over and kissed his cheek. "Thank you so much, Dante!"

He smiled happily. "You're welcome, angel."

"Wait, how did you know I love football?"

"I asked Dmitri about you the day I met you. He mentioned you used to play the sport, so I figured you might like to watch a game."

"Oh man, this is going to be so great! The Niners are playing Seattle tonight." I actually bounced up and down in my seat a little. I knew I was acting like a three-year-old, but I couldn't help myself.

"Yes. The Seattle Seahawks."

I turned to look at his profile as he wove through traffic, and grinned. "Did you have to Google that?"

He grinned too and admitted, "Maybe."

*****

We had the best seats in the house. Literally. Dante had gotten us a private skybox, something I'd only ever dreamt of. "I've died and gone to heaven," I murmured as I sunk into the plush seat and looked out over the field with a huge smile. "I feel like the king of football in here."

Dante also had a big smile on his face. "I've never seen anyone so happy about anything."

"This is just the absolute best," I gushed. "You're the absolute best." I took his face between my hands and kissed him, then leapt up and explored the skybox. In addition to the comfy seating, there was a private bathroom, a stocked bar, and a full buffet. "There's no reason to ever leave," I said happily as I picked up a little cube of cheese and popped it in my mouth.

"I agree," Dante said, coming up behind me and wrapping his arms around my waist.

I leaned back against him and put a cheese cube in his mouth. "Thank you so much for doing this for me. We didn't have to be this fancy, though. I would have been perfectly happy even with nosebleed seats."

"This is far more private, though," he said as he slipped his hand under my polo shirt and caressed my belly.

"That's a good point." I pivoted around in his arms and kissed him passionately.

The announcer's voice came over a hidden loudspeaker, and I quickly made up a plate at the buffet and took my seat.

Dante grabbed a couple cold beers out of a mini fridge and told me as he sat down beside me, "If you want anything from the regular concessions, we can call the concierge. He'll bring you whatever you want."

"Heaven. Absolute heaven," I murmured, and put my head on Dante's shoulder as I picked up his hand.

"I've never known anyone who liked a sport so much. I've never known anyone who liked *anything* so much," Dante said.

"It's not just a sport. It's *football*."

He grinned at that. "So, you played in high school?"

"Yup, all four years. College, too. For three whole weeks, anyway. I went to Stanford on a full football scholarship. But I destroyed my knee not even a month into my freshman year, and came right back home again."

"God, I'm sorry," he said.

I just shrugged. "It is what it is. I've had a few years to get over it."

"What position did you play?"

"Tight end."

A huge smile spread across Dante's face. "You're shitting me. That's not a real position, is it?"

I burst out laughing. "Wow. You seriously do not know jack shit about football!"

"No, I really don't. Now tell me, is that a real position?"

I just started laughing again, so Dante pulled out his phone. After a minute of tapping on his screen, he said, "Well, I'll be damned."

That just made me laugh even more. Then I joked, "So, what will you be doing for the next three hours while I watch the game?"

"I'll be watching you watch the game." He looked pleased with that prospect.

"Oh no. See, if you're going to hang with me, it's vitally important that you learn to love football. You don't have to love it as much as I do, but you *do* have to love it. And that means actually watching the game."

I'd been teasing him, but he looked concerned and pulled out his phone again. After a couple taps on the screen, he read, "Each team gets four tries, or 'downs' to—"

I plucked the phone out of his hands and kissed him before telling him, "You don't need that. You have me."

"Oh no. I'm not going to distract you with my stupid questions. I want you to enjoy the game."

I snuggled against him and said, "Oh I will, guaranteed." The teams were taking the field, and I picked up his hand and said quietly, "I'm so glad you brought me here. I used to come here all the time with my dad, and later with Jamie. There are a lot of bittersweet memories in this stadium. I'm glad I'm making new memories with you." He smiled at me before turning his attention to the field.

Dante tried hard to feign interest throughout the first half. I thought that was incredibly sweet. At halftime, he turned to me with a rehearsed blank expression and asked, "Who's winning?" He smiled at me cheerfully. I smiled too and planted a big kiss on his lips. Then he asked, "How long do we have for intermission?"

"Halftime, not intermission. We have about fifteen minutes."

"That's it?"

"Yup."

"Okay, I can make it work," Dante said with a big grin, standing up and pulling me to my feet with him.

"Make what work?" I asked as he towed me into the private bathroom and closed the door behind us.

"I want to make sure this is your best experience ever at this stadium," he said as he got on his knees in front of me.

"Oh holy shit," I murmured. He unzipped my jeans and slid them and my boxer briefs down to mid-thigh, then licked my cock. It instantly sprang to attention. "Wow, are you really going to...ahhhh," I moaned as he took my cock to its base and sucked me, gently at first, but soon with increasing urgency.

In just a matter of minutes I was yelling and shooting down his throat, both hands braced on the walls of the bathroom. Dante kept sucking me as he caressed my balls, and when I finally finished, he pulled up my underwear and jeans and zipped me up again. Then he stood up and glanced at his watch. "Eleven minutes," he said with a satisfied grin. He winked at me and left the restroom.

It was a solid minute before my legs stopped shaking and I could actually follow him back to our seats. When I sank down beside him, I pulled him to me and kissed him, and then I said, "The score is two-zip."

"No it's not. It's fourteen-six, Forty Niners."

"Not the football game," I said with a smile. "You've now made me cum twice, and I have yet to reciprocate."

"I'm not keeping score."

"I am."

"Game's about to start," Dante said, tilting his head toward the field.

"I know. I don't care." I slid my fingers up his thigh.

He scooped up my hand and kissed it. "Yes you do. No way am I letting you miss a minute of this game."

I sighed and said, "Fine. But tonight, I want a chance to even the score." I tucked my feet up onto my seat and put my head on his shoulder, still holding his hand. After a minute I asked, "I'm curious why you did that in there and not out here. This is really private, no one's at the right angle to see in."

"No one except for the TV cameras with their zoom lenses. Haven't you ever noticed the shots of celebrities and VIPs inside the skyboxes during televised sporting events?"

"Oh." I sat up straight for a moment. "That didn't occur to me." I mulled it over for a moment, then put my head back on his shoulder. "Wait, you don't watch football. How did you know about that?"

"I Googled 'how private is a skybox at an NFL game' beforehand. You know, just in case we decided to do what we just did."

I was still chuckling as the second half got under way.

*****

That night when we finally returned to my apartment (following a Niners victory!), I was randy as hell and determined to even the score. I pushed Dante up against the wall of my apartment and kissed him deeply, and when we finally broke apart, he smiled and plucked the big foam finger off my right hand. Before leaving the stadium, he'd loaded me up with souvenirs. Apparently he was under the impression that I'd actually need stuff to remember the best night of my entire life.

He pulled my new Niners sweatshirt off over my head, and my polo shirt came off along with it. He then peppered my shoulders and chest with kisses and sexy little nips as his hands moved to my jeans. Dante somehow got me stripped completely naked in under a minute, and once again, he remained clothed. He maneuvered me to the bed as he continued to kiss and caress and nibble on me, and we fell back with him on top of me as his thigh slid between my legs, parting them. I rolled over on top of him and said, "It's my turn to pleasure you tonight," as I pulled both his sweater and t-shirt off over his head. "Oh wow," I murmured appreciatively, at the sight of his big, muscular body, his olive skin golden in the soft light. I dipped my head down to kiss and lick his neck and shoulders.

He ran his hands down my back and cupped my ass, squeezing it gently. Then he spread me slightly and traced a fingertip between my cheeks, grazing the outside of my opening. That had me up like a shot. Before I even realized what I was doing, I was standing a couple feet away from the bed, fidgeting nervously. Dante propped himself up on his elbows and gave me a little half-smile as he said, "So, I take it you don't like that."

"Um...I don't know. I could like that, I suppose, if it didn't scare the bajeezus out of me." God, I sounded like an idiot.

He sat up and said, "I assume that means you've never bottomed before."

"I've never topped, either," I admitted. I knew it made me sound hopelessly naïve to be this inexperienced at my age, but I had to be honest with him.

Dante slid out of bed and took me in his arms, hugging me gently. "So, you and Jamie never...."

"Got farther than oral."

He was quiet for a few moments, processing this information. Then he asked gently, "How far are you planning to go with me, angel?"

"As far as you're willing to take me." I was almost dizzy with panic, but I was absolutely determined to overcome my fear.

"We can take this really slowly, Charlie. I wasn't planning to have sex with you tonight anyway. I was just going to finger you."

My body shook when he said that, fear and arousal wrapped up one in the other. It took some effort to find my voice again, and finally I managed, "I've...um...I've never had anything in me." Damn, there was that hopelessly naïve thing again.

He paused once more, probably trying to make sense of me. After a moment he asked softly, "Would you let me penetrate you?" All I could manage was a nod. "That scares the hell out of you," he observed quietly. "But you'd still let me do that to you?" Another nod. I held on to him tightly and kissed his shoulder. My entire body was still trembling. God, he must think I was a complete basket case.

I just couldn't explain it to him. I couldn't find the words to tell him how much sex had always terrified me, how the idea of being penetrated, even though a part of me longed for it, filled me with fear and panic. Well, I probably didn't actually need to explain it to him. He was seeing it for himself.

"Do you want to try that tonight? Or do you want to wait?" He was so sweet, so patient.

"Please," I began, before my voice ran out.

"Please wait?" he guessed.

I shook my head no, and made myself say, "I don't want to wait. I want this."

He pulled back to look at me, and caressed my cheek. "Are you sure? If you're not ready, there's no hurry."

"I need to do this," I whispered as I hugged him to me. "I need to get past my fear, and I know you won't hurt me."

He held me for a long moment, and then he took my hand and brought me back to the bed. I lay down on my back and looked up at him, swallowing against the tightness in my throat. "I'm going to get a couple things, angel. You wait here." He went into the bathroom.

I got up and pulled aside the big, downy comforter, then crawled back into bed, lying on the soft, dark blue sheets on my stomach, hands beneath my head. *You can do this*, I told myself, trying to give myself a pep talk. *So what if you're afraid? That's not an excuse anymore, remember?*

Dante was back a minute later, and set a couple things on the mattress as he sat beside me, so close that his hip rested against my side. The contact was a comfort, and I reached out and caressed his bare thigh. He'd stripped down to just a pair of boxers. He stroked my back gently, soothingly, and he said softly, "I think you'd like this best if I was holding you while I fingered you."

I nodded in agreement and slid over, and he climbed into bed and lay back against the pillows. I wasn't sure what to do, but he held his arms out to me and I crawled on top of him, straddling his thighs and laying down on his chest, most of my weight on my knees and elbows. He wrapped his strong arms around me, holding me securely. "You sure you want to do this tonight, Charlie?" His voice was so soft.

"Yes. You're going to take good care of me. I know you will."

"Oh angel," he whispered. I raised myself up and my mouth found his, and he kissed me deeply. I parted my lips for him and his tongue stroked mine as arousal stirred deep within me.

After a few minutes of kissing and caressing, his hand slid down my back, his movements slow and intentional. He was trying not to startle me. My heart flip-flopped as he took hold of one of my cheeks and spread me gently. The fingertips of his other hand massaged up and down my crack, grazing over my opening. *Just breathe*, I told myself, as his fingertip began to lightly circle my hole.

Dante kept this up for a while, and as I calmed down a little I marveled at his patience. Finally, he picked up something from the mattress, and I turned my head to see what he was doing. He held up a pump bottle of lotion where I could see it, one arm around my waist. Deftly, with one hand, he dispensed a little lotion into his palm, then put the bottle back down and closed his hand around the white liquid. It occurred to me after a moment that he was warming it up.

He slid his other hand back down to my butt and spread me again, and I wrapped my arms tightly around his shoulders. I felt the cream being applied to my opening, and then he was gently pushing inside me. A little sound escaped me, almost a whimper, and I probably would have been mortified at that if I'd had the capacity to be anything besides terrified just then.

When just his fingertip was in me, he held his hand still and let me get used to it. Then slowly, so slowly, he worked his finger into me. I went right on clinging to him, my face pressed into his shoulder, taking comfort in him. Maybe that was odd, since he was actually what was causing me distress.

Once his finger was deep inside me, he held his hand still again and asked softly, "You doing okay, Charlie?" When I nodded, he started sliding his finger in and out of me. It felt…good, I realized. Really, really good.

It was a revelation, and I exhaled slowly. I hadn't even been aware that I'd been holding my breath. My body relaxed on top of this, and I slid my knees apart, allowing him better access to me.

When he felt me relax, Dante began working my hole a little harder, twisting his finger around inside me. I gasped with surprise and jumped a little when he grazed my prostate and sent a jolt of pleasure through my body. "Do you like that?" he whispered.

"Yes." I moaned when he found that spot again and began rubbing it. Oh God, it was *so good*, and it was a turning point, fear totally crowded out by lust. I braced my hands on the headboard and rocked back onto his hand, trying to take him deeper, and he started fingering me a little harder.

I threw my head back and bucked on his hand, and in the next moment I was crying out and cumming all over Dante's chest and stomach, my rock hard cock totally untouched. I just kept spurting and spurting, and he kept milking me by rubbing that spot inside me. I think I was yelling, "Yes, yes," as he worked me, carrying me through to the end of my orgasm.

When finally it ebbed, he eased out of me slowly, carefully, and I collapsed on top of him, sweaty and gasping for breath. "Oh God…that was…so intense," I managed between gasps.

I was totally spent after that, and Dante rolled me onto my back. He picked up a towel that he'd brought from the bathroom and wiped the cum from my body, then swiped a clean corner of the towel over my opening. It was a surprisingly intimate gesture, and I laughed nervously. That was probably silly, considering how intimate we'd been just moments before.

He went to the bathroom and cleaned himself up, and by the time he got back to bed, although it was only a minute later, I was almost asleep. But I pried my eyes open as he gathered me into his arms, and I murmured, "Damn it. Three-zip."

He chuckled softly and said, "I'm still not keeping score."

I nestled against him and whispered, "Thank you for doing that for me, and for being so patient and understanding. I was so afraid of that, but it ended up being so good."

Dante pulled the blanket up to my shoulders and kissed the top of my head, and I wrapped my arms around him tightly as he said, "It was my pleasure."

"You're wonderful," I murmured, sleep closing fast. "You make me feel so good. And I'm not just talking about sex." I nuzzled his shoulder and told him softly, "I've never felt more safe or secure than I do right at this very moment."

And right before I fell asleep, Dante whispered, "Neither have I."

Chapter Six

I was pleasantly surprised to find Dante in my kitchen the next morning, and I exclaimed, "You stayed!"

He smiled apologetically and said, "Well, no. I went home after you fell asleep. But I borrowed your keys and let myself back in this morning. I hope that's okay."

I crossed the room to him, grabbed him in a hug and smiled up at him as I said, "It's so much better than okay." He kissed me and I sank into it before realizing I hadn't brushed my teeth yet. I stepped back self-consciously and noticed that he was showered and neatly dressed in black pants and a black button-down shirt, the collar open and the cuffs rolled back. "God you look sexy," I murmured, before turning and fleeing to the bathroom. "Don't go anywhere," I called over my shoulder. "I'll be out in a minute."

I brushed my teeth and showered quickly, then hurried back to the kitchen wearing nothing but a towel. "You're cooking," I said with a grin as I jumped up on the counter and watched what he was doing. He was chopping vegetables with chef-like dexterity, the knife a blur in his big hand. "And judging by those knife skills, you look like you're really good at it."

He grinned and said, "I don't know about that. I just enjoy it. You can tell me if I'm any good after you taste this omelet."

I reached into the cupboard behind me, pulled out a mug, and poured myself some coffee as I watched him. "There's something so hot about a man who can cook," I said.

"There is?"

"Definitely."

"Do you cook?"

I took a sip of coffee, then said, "Oh yeah. I make a mean Pop Tart. And I can pour a bowl of cereal like nobody's business."

He smiled at that, then kissed my forehead on his way to the stove. "In that case, you can make breakfast tomorrow."

"Deal."

There was a (new) skillet heating on the stovetop, and he slid the vegetables off the cutting board into the pan, then grabbed the handle and tossed the pan's contents in the air a couple times, coating them in olive oil. "Okay, that's it. This is officially totally unbalanced," I said as I hopped off the counter, came up behind him and slid my arms around his waist. "You've bought me furniture, you've taken me out, and our sex score stands at three-zip. Now on top of that, it turns out you have mad skills in the kitchen. I bring nothing to this relationship."

He turned to face me and kissed me sweetly. "You bring me to life, Charlie," he told me, resting his hands on my waist. He added, a little sparkle in his eyes, "Besides, you took me out once and I took you out once, so on that score, we're completely even."

I laughed at that. "Oh my God. Are you comparing me taking you to break in to my parents' house to you taking me to a luxury box at the Stick?" He nodded, and I laughed again.

"Actually, the date you took me on was much more fun," he said with a smile. "There wasn't a single killer zombie lap dog at the football game."

I ran my hand down his back and said, "Can't I at least even up the sex score? God knows I can't cook or buy you furniture, so this is pretty much my one shot at evening us up a bit." I smiled at him cheerfully.

He paused for a long moment, chewing on his bottom lip, then said, "Actually, you and I need to talk about the whole sex thing, Charlie. There's a lot you need to know about me."

"Oh yeah?" I said, raising my eyebrows. "Are you into all sorts of freaky stuff, so sex with you needs to come with a disclaimer?"

I'd been kidding, of course. But he broke my gaze and said, "Pretty much."

Dante turned away from me, pulled the skillet from the burner and turned off the heat. He kept his back to me for a long moment, and I asked, "Seriously?"

When he turned back to face me, he said, his voice low, "I really should have told you this earlier. But I was having so much fun, and I wanted just a little more time with you. I didn't want to scare you away so soon."

"You think you're going to scare me away?"

"It's a given, especially because I realized last night just how incredibly innocent you are."

I met Dante's gaze. There was such sorrow and such raw vulnerability in his eyes. It seemed totally unlike him. How many people, if any, had ever been allowed to look past his veneer, to see this part of him? I said quietly, "Please don't make assumptions. Just talk to me."

He looked down at the floor for a very long moment. When he looked back up at me, he'd managed to pull his veneer back in place, any signs of vulnerability safely tucked out of sight. He seemed to be kind of bracing himself, squaring his shoulders, his jaw set. It occurred to me that he was preparing himself for my rejection, getting ready for me to balk, to…what exactly? Laugh at him? Be disgusted by him? I really didn't know what he thought was going to happen here.

When he spoke, his tone was low and level as he said, "Whenever I fuck someone, I need them bound, immobile, totally under my control. And before I fuck them, I need to beat the person I'm with. At the very least, I need to spank them, hard. But I really get off on whipping them. I literally…" he took a deep breath. "I literally can't have sex any other way."

I mulled this over for a long moment. Panic had of course welled up in me when he told me that, and my heart was racing. But right along with it was something else, something stronger: an aching desire. A need, for what exactly, I didn't know. I took his hand and said, "Show me."

He looked up at me, startled. "Show you what, exactly?"

"Show me exactly what you need. Beat me. Tie me up and fuck me. Don't hold back. I need to know if I can handle it."

"How can I do that to you, Charlie?" he asked incredulously. "I care about you."

A little half-smile tugged the corner of my lips, and I asked, "Haven't you ever cared about a sex partner before?"

"No. Not even a little."

"Oh." That answer startled and saddened me. After a moment, I said, "So, I guess it'll be a first for both of us, then."

He blinked at me in surprise. "Why on earth would you agree to this?"

"Because I want you, Dante. If this is what it takes in order to be with you, then I'm certainly willing to try it."

"Charlie...."

"Do these things give you pleasure, Dante? Whipping someone? Tying them up?"

There was raw emotion in his voice when he said, "Yes."

"I want to give you pleasure. God I want that. Please let me."

"I'm sorry, angel," he whispered. I thought he was going to turn and walk away.

But in the next instant he was shoving me up against the cabinet, his mouth claiming mine in a brutal kiss. He pulled the towel off my hips, grabbed my wrists and slammed my hands against the cabinet, holding me in place. My lips parted under his and he tasted my mouth, his big, powerful body pressing against me, pinning me down.

"Oh God, yes Dante," I moaned as he bit my earlobe, my entire body coming alive, practically humming with desire.

He swung me onto the kitchen floor and climbed on top of me, holding my hands down on either side of my head, his fingers laced with mine. His thigh parted my legs as he claimed my mouth again and I cried out against his lips, my hard cock pressed against him.

There was no time to psych myself out, no room for panic, no chance for fear to take over. There was only blinding desire and Dante, taking what he needed, and I gave myself over to it entirely. To *him* entirely.

He was like a different person, powerful, confident, commanding. I saw then just how much he'd been holding back, how careful he'd been with me these last couple days. Everything before this point had been just for me, to make me comfortable and to make me feel good. Now I so desperately wanted him to feel good, too.

Dante brought me up into a seated position, took hold of my hair and pulled my head back. He kissed and licked my neck before moving down my body and biting my nipples, not hard enough to break the skin, but not soft, either. Then he pulled back just a couple inches, passion burning in the depths of his dark eyes. "Are you sure? Are you absolutely positive you want to do this, Charlie?"

"Yes. God yes. Please let me pleasure you, Dante."

With a deep breath, he swung me face down across his lap. Then he brought his hand down on my ass. Hard.

The sound that tore from me was as much a moan as a yell. He grasped my arm and pinned it behind my back, using it to hold me in place on his lap as he spanked me again, another hard slap. And another. I bucked on his lap but made no effort to escape.

Instead, I gave myself over to it, to the pain, to pure, raw sex, to intense, forbidden pleasure as a part of me I'd never been aware of took over, surrendering myself to this man, to his needs. To *my* needs.

God I needed this.

Again and again he beat my ass, the pain crescendoing as my moans and yells turned into something wild, primal. After a while I realized he was moaning too, his cock rock hard and pressing against me as I lay across his lap.

I was sure I was going to cum just like that, just from the beating he was giving me. But abruptly, he stopped hitting me and rolled me onto my back on the floor. He grabbed both of my wrists, holding them in one of his hands, and yanked my arms up over my head. With his other hand, he unbuckled his leather belt and pulled it free, then used it to bind my hands together. He fastened the loose end around one of the legs of the wrought iron table, and as soon as I was secured, he grabbed something off the kitchen counter.

He held a glass bottle of olive oil and drizzled some over my cock and balls, then took hold of my hard shaft and started pumping me, the oil acting as lubricant. He freed his straining cock from his pants and boxers and started stroking himself as well, kneeling between my spread legs, and I realized he intended to finish us off this way. I begged shamelessly, my voice shaking, "Please Dante, take me. Fuck me. I need you in me. Please." My fear was totally forgotten. I was that completely aroused, that caught up in the moment.

But instead of fucking me as I'd expected, he released my cock and pushed two oil-slicked fingers inside me. I gasped at the sudden penetration. He finger fucked me quickly, roughly, and when I was about to cum he dropped down between my legs and took my cock down his throat as he continued to work my hole. It only took a few hard sucks and then I was yelling as I came, bucking into his mouth, pulling against my restraints.

Just as my orgasm finally began to ebb, he released my cock from his mouth and got up on his knees between my legs. He yelled as he shot his load all over my naked body and went right on finger fucking me, milking my cum out of me as I moaned and writhed.

When we were both finally spent, he pulled his fingers out of me carefully. He crawled around beside me and kissed me tenderly, then sat up and said, "I couldn't fuck you. God I wanted to. But I would have torn you open. There was no way I could have been patient and prepared you enough, not while I was that aroused."

"Thank you for taking care of me, Dante."

His concerned dark eyes searched my face. "I was still pretty rough with you. Are you okay?"

"Better than okay." I smiled up at him and said, "That was absolutely amazing."

He grinned at me. "You actually liked it?"

I chuckled and said, "Really? My rock hard cock wasn't enough of an indicator of just how much I loved that? You have to ask?"

He quickly washed his hands and dried them on a paper towel, then lightly ran a caress down my body. I was still bound to the table, totally naked, totally exposed. But I felt so good that it didn't bother me in the least. "You continually astound me, angel," he said softly.

"So do you." I was grinning happily.

He leaned in and kissed me again, then said, "I'll untie you in a minute. I just want to savor the sight of you like this a little longer." He looked so happy, so content as he smiled down at me and brushed back my hair.

"I'm in no hurry," I murmured. He went back to exploring my body, lightly caressing, tracing the lines of my abs, then rolling my nipple between two fingers, hardening into a little bead as my cock jumped. I said, "You know, I'm still tied up. If you felt like going for round two, I certainly wouldn't object."

"It's amazing that you're so relaxed and okay with all of this."

"I guess I always just needed someone to take control. Turns out I don't panic when I'm caught up in the moment and someone else is guiding me."

Just then someone knocked on the front door. I frowned at that, and Dante said, "If we don't answer, maybe they'll go away," before rolling my other nipple between his fingers.

A woman's voice called out, "Charlie? Are you in there?" I think I stopped breathing for a moment, my heart stuttering, my eyes going wide.

Dante saw my reaction and asked, "Who is that?"

I said, very quietly, "It's my mother."

Chapter Seven

"Oh shit!" he exclaimed, and quickly unfastened the belt from around my wrists. He stood up and began straightening his clothes, tucking his shirt in, zipping his pants as I sat up and stared dumbfounded at the front door, directly in my line of sight past the kitchen and living room.

"What's she doing here?" I murmured.

"Want me to tell her to leave?" Dante asked, holding his hand out to me. I took it automatically, and he pulled me to my feet.

"No. It must be important. She wouldn't come here otherwise." I was a bit dazed as I looked down at myself. I was completely naked, my cock slick with oil, Dante's cum all over my body. "Fuck," I whispered, realizing the state I was in.

"Go get in the shower. I'll let her in if you want me to, and stall her while you get yourself together," Dante told me as he ran his belt around his waist and buckled it in place.

I nodded and did as I was told, padding naked through the kitchen and living room, then stepping through my bedroom door and closing and locking it behind me. I went into the bathroom and turned on the shower, then got under the water and washed myself with shaking hands.

What was she doing here? Had she figured out I'd broken into her house, and was she here to have me arrested?

I didn't think she was here to reconcile, not after the way they'd weeded me out of their lives and tried to throw away every sign I'd ever existed.

I shut off the water after a couple minutes and stepped out of the shower. I dried myself quickly and ran a comb through my wet hair, then went to the bedroom and got dressed. As I was tying my shoes, I noticed something, and it brought me up short. Both of my wrists were red and chafed from the way I'd pulled against the belt. Oh God. How was I going to explain that to my mother? How would I explain that to anyone? It was too private to put it out there for the world to see. After thinking for a moment, I pulled on my new, oversized Forty Niners sweatshirt and tugged the sleeves down to my knuckles before taking a deep breath and leaving the bedroom.

Dante and my mother were seated in the kitchen. She was sobbing into one of his monogrammed handkerchiefs. As I came into the room I almost stepped on Peaches, who got up from the floor and growled at me, his hackles rising. I ignored him, and he went and sat by my mother.

As soon as she caught sight of me, her wailing increased tenfold, and she pushed up off the chair and crossed the room to me quickly, grabbing me in a hug. I went completely rigid. "Oh Charlie," she cried, crushing me to her. "I'm so sorry. It wasn't my idea. I just want you to know that. None of it was my idea. It was all your father's doing. I don't care that you're gay. I don't."

"Has something happened?"

She let go of me and blew her nose in Dante's handkerchief, then said, "I've left your father."

"But…you're Catholic. You don't actually believe in divorce," I pointed out, totally dumbfounded.

She shrugged and pushed her blonde hair back from her face. My mother was in her late fifties and had long since stopped making an effort with her appearance. The one exception was her hair, which she colored platinum blonde in an act of vanity I'd never been able to grasp. "So, I'm not going to divorce him. But I'm not going to live with him anymore, either." She took a couple deep breaths, and Dante came up to us and handed her a glass of water. She accepted it with a warm, "Thank you, Dante," then drank half of it before coming up for air.

"Why don't you sit back down, Mrs. Connolly?" Dante said. He was being unfailingly polite, but his eyes were wary.

She returned to one of the kitchen chairs, and I remained rooted where I was. I said, "If you don't care that I'm gay, why didn't you say something sooner? Why did you let him throw me out, and then eliminate every trace of me from your house?"

"What could I say? You know how your father is."

"Gee, I don't know. How about, *stop, he's our son. We shouldn't do this to him.*" I crossed my arms over my chest.

"Charlie, I'm so sorry. I was weak, I didn't know how to stand up to him. I wanted to go with you when he threw you out, but you know I don't have my own money, I didn't know what to do. I was at his mercy."

"So, how are you leaving him now?"

"I called my sister Joan in Dayton. She mailed me money for a plane ticket. It got here yesterday, and today when your father went to the post office, I packed a bag and Peaches and I took off." She sat up a little straighter and said, "I left him a note. It said *this is for what you did to Charlie.*"

"Great, *now* you have my back," I muttered.

"I didn't know if I'd be able to get out of there, Charlie. I didn't know if my sister would send me the money for the plane ticket."

"Where are you going?"

"To Ohio, to live with Joan. She's a widow now, she's got plenty of room. The farther I can get from your father, the better." She looked up at me, her green eyes red from crying. "I just came to say goodbye, Charlie. I'm on my way to the airport."

"Okay. Well, see ya."

But then she burst into tears again. "Aw gawd Charlie, please don't hate me. I couldn't bear it if my only son hated me."

I just couldn't take her tears. Even as hurt and angry as I was, they wore me down, and after a while I crossed the kitchen to her and patted her shoulder. "Come on, Ma. Don't cry. I don't hate you."

She jumped up and crushed me in another hug, and it was a good couple minutes before she finally stopped crying. Dante was ready with another clean handkerchief, and she took it from him when she let go of me and thanked him, then told me, "I'm glad you found yourself such a nice boyfriend, Charlie. So handsome and polite." To Dante she said, "You make sure you take care of my son, you hear?"

"Count on it," he said quietly.

She wiped her eyes with the handkerchief, then straightened her old brown wool coat. "I'm going to need to get going soon, Charlie," she said. "I got one of those airport shuttles coming to pick me up downstairs. But before I go, I have a favor to ask you."

Really? I resisted the urge to roll my eyes, and said, "What is it, Ma?"

She hesitated for a long moment, biting the inside of her cheek. It was an odd habit of hers. Finally she said, "So, you know Aunt Joan has eleven cats."

"I knew she had some. I didn't know she had eleven."

My mother paused again, then said, "She told me I could only come live with her on one condition. She told me I couldn't bring Peaches."

"So, why didn't you leave him with Dad?"

"Because your father would take him straight to the pound!"

"Okay. So why are you telling me this?" Then understanding dawned on me, and I said, "Wait a minute, you can't possibly think that I—"

"Please Charlie? Please take Peaches. I know you'll take care of him. I love him so much. I just can't let him be put down!" She looked up at me with huge eyes, tears rolling down her cheeks.

"That dog hates me, Ma. You know that. He wouldn't be happy here."

"There's no one else I can turn to, Charlie!"

"What about Uncle Al? He has a house with a yard. The dog would be much happier there."

"Your father's brother is an asshole," my mother informed me. It was the first time I'd ever heard her swear. "He'd put Peaches down faster than you could say euthanasia. Please Charlie? Won't you do this for me?"

I wanted to say no. God I wanted to. But I just couldn't do that to her. I knew exactly what that dog meant to her, and I couldn't let him be put down. After a long few moments, during which I desperately tried and failed to come up with another solution, *any* other solution, I sighed and said, "Fine."

Dante's eyes went wide behind my mother, and he stared at me like I'd completely lost my mind, shaking his head no almost frantically. "I knew I could count on you, Charlie," she said with a big smile. "Well, I better get downstairs, I don't want to miss that shuttle." My mother bustled to the front door, giving me instructions as she went. "Don't forget to give Peaches his special dog food. There's a bag of his things here by the door. And make sure you change his water twice a day, he only likes it fresh."

Peaches followed us to the front door, wagging his stumpy tail happily. Then my mother burst into tears again. But instead of hugging me, she dropped to her knees and hugged the dog. "Goodbye, Peaches. Mama loves you. Your brother Charlie's gonna take good care of you, baby. Mama's so sorry."

This went on for a few minutes, and finally she put the dog down and picked up her pink suitcase. She said, "I'll write to you from Dayton, Charlie. You take care of yourself. It was a pleasure meeting you, Dante." She opened the door and stepped out into the hall, then remembered something and said, "Oh, just so you know, Peaches has a bit of diarrhea. I don't know why. Should clear up in a day or two, I'd imagine." With those parting words, my mother turned and walked away.

I closed the door behind her, and turned to Dante and pointed an accusing finger. "You just *had* to give Peaches the buns. Now look! Talk about karma!"

The dog was staring at the closed front door dejectedly, his tail and ears drooping. My heart went out to the little guy, who'd just lost his owner and looked so small and pathetic. I went to pet him, console him a bit, and Peaches whirled on me, his underbite revealed as he bared his teeth and growled.

"No!" I said that so sharply that Peaches was startled enough to actually stop growling. "What are you complaining about?" I asked him. "You got more of a heartfelt goodbye than I did. You should feel lucky."

His response to that was to raise his hackles and bare his teeth again, a high-pitched growl coming from his throat.

"Fuck my life," I said, scrubbing my hands over my face.

"That's it. I'm taking that little fucker to the pound," Dante told me as he went to grab the dog. It almost took a chunk out of his hand, and Dante swore vividly as he jumped back and exclaimed, "The little bastard tried to bite me!"

"Of course he did. You tried to pick him up."

Dante pulled his phone out of his pocket. "I'm calling animal control, and telling them to bring a dart gun."

I sighed and said, "It's fine. Let him stay." I went to the kitchen and poured myself another cup of coffee, the dog following, growling and snapping at my heels the whole way.

"Are you nuts? You can't let that hellhound terrorize you in your own home!"

"It's just temporary, until I figure out what to do with him."

"I already know what to do with him. It's called *the pound!*"

"I'm such a sucker," I said with a sigh, talking a little loudly over the constant growl of the smelly canine at my feet. "Probably the only reason my mother even came here and made amends was so I'd take Peaches in." The dog tried to lunge for my leg, but I got my sneaker up in time and pivoted around, shielding myself. "I know she's not leaving my father because he kicked me out. She's leaving him because they have a miserable relationship, and is using this as an excuse to do what she's probably wanted to do for years."

Dante knit his brows for a moment, then pretended to be reasonable as he said, "Let me take him to my house. I have a fenced yard, he can stay there."

"Are you going to shoot him as soon as you get him home?"

"No."

"Are you going to shoot him *before* you get him home?" Dante looked guilty, and I said, "Thought so." I noticed the clock on the stove and sighed. "Damn it. I need to be at work in fifteen minutes."

"I'll take care of the dog," Dante told me. "You go ahead and go."

"That's what I'm afraid of, that you'll *take care of the dog.*"

"I'm not going to shoot him. Not if you don't want me to. I'll just keep an eye on him for you."

"You don't have to stay with the dog," I told him, loudly, over the constant growling. "We can just lock him up in here until I get home."

"He'll destroy the entire apartment if we do that," Dante said. "I don't have any pressing business to take care of today anyway, so I can stay."

"Are you sure?"

"Yes. Go to work, Charlie."

I hesitated for a long moment. I really couldn't blow off my job, I'd only been working there a few days and didn't want Jamie to think I was a total flake. And Dante had a point about the dog destroying everything in sight. "Well, okay." I grabbed my wallet and keys, and Dante walked me to the front door and kissed my forehead.

The dog let out a long, moist-sounding fart, and I pressed my eyes shut and said, "That would be the gluten sensitivity. The diarrhea train's going to be pulling into the station sometime in the next two minutes. I'd better call in to work."

"Don't worry. I've got this."

"Seriously?"

"Karma's a bitch," Dante said with a little grin, and pushed me out the door.

"Don't kill the dog!" I called over my shoulder as I hurried down the hall.

Chapter Eight

Okay, so that had been pretty mean of me, leaving Dante with the dog from hell while I went off to work. I'd texted him repeatedly during my shift, and he kept assuring me that everything was going fine. Still, I braced myself as I pushed open the door to my apartment four hours later. Since I wasn't immediately rushed by a crazed canine, I stepped into the apartment calling, "Aw man! You killed the dog, didn't you?"

My living room was filled with gorgeous furniture, but I turned my attention to Dante instead. He was coming out of the kitchen dressed in an old practice jersey and sweat pants of mine, both of which were soaking wet. He was barefoot, his dark hair tousled, and he wore huge leather gloves on each hand that extended up to his elbows. "Are those blacksmithing gloves?" I asked, trying to keep a straight face.

"Falconry, actually." He put his gloved hands on his hips, a grin on his face. "Go ahead. Laugh. I know you're dying to."

"Nah. It's too mean." I crossed the room to him and kissed him, then stepped back and said, "Oh boy."

Dante frowned at me. "I smell like wet dog, don't I?"

"Big time. Don't tell me you drowned Peaches in the bathtub."

"I wish. But no, I washed the disgusting little zombie instead. I couldn't take the smell."

"The bath didn't help at all, did it?"

"Not even a little."

"Told you that smell was his breath. So where is the little shit?"

"He's in his pen," Dante said, inclining his head toward the kitchen.

"He has a pen?"

"Yup."

"What kind of pen?"

"I think it's meant to hold small livestock," he told me.

"And you found a livestock pen where?"

"Same place I found the gloves," Dante said as he tried to peel one off with some effort. Apparently falconry gloves shrunk if you got them wet.

I went into the kitchen and surveyed the situation. The whole room reeked of wet dog. Peaches was damp and dejected, behind bars in a little metal corral in the breakfast nook, the kitchen floor beneath him lined with some type of disposable kennel pads. There was a space heater pointed at him from outside the corral, and the window was open to let out some of the smell. I grinned and turned to Dante. "How did you do all of this? Did you leave Peaches unattended after all while you went and ran these errands?"

"I couldn't, he'd destroy your home. I researched this stuff online, then texted a couple of my men and they picked up the supplies."

"You have men?"

"Employees." Dante swore and gave one of the gloves a hard yank, and finally it peeled off.

"Yeah, I get that part," I said with a grin. "Is the kitchen table in the living room now? I didn't notice."

"It is."

"Along with an awful lot of new furniture."

"I told you I had stuff on backorder for you." He tugged hard, cursed vividly, and finally pulled the other glove off. I fought back a laugh.

"So, all the backorder stuff got here today?"

"No. I cancelled that order and had my men bring different stuff. I couldn't wait. I needed a place to collapse after a hard day of zombie lap dog wrestling."

"You'd better not collapse on my new couch smelling like that!" I told him. Then I gave him a big smile.

"Oh, that's it," Dante exclaimed, and grabbed me in a hug. "If I have to smell like wet dog, then so do you." He planted kisses all over my face.

"Ew, quit it!" I yelled, laughing and struggling to get away as the dampness from his clothes soaked through mine.

We both needed a shower after that, and decided to take one together. Dante kissed me as we stripped and got under the warm spray, and he soaped his hands up and washed my shoulders and belly. When I turned around so he could do my back, he whispered, "Shit."

I turned around to look at him. "What's wrong?"

"Your butt's bruised," he said quietly. "Does it hurt?"

"A little, but I don't mind."

"I'm so sorry."

"Don't be. I loved being spanked. It was incredibly arousing." I took the soap from him and lathered up my hands, then ran them over his broad chest.

"I was really holding back," he said after a minute. That surprised me. I hadn't thought he was holding back at all.

"You didn't have to. I liked it, Dante. A lot."

"Maybe that's just because you're used to people treating you like crap."

"What?"

"Your family's horrible, Charlie. That had to have messed with your self-esteem. So, I don't know. Maybe you think you deserve this, to be beaten, to be treated this way. But you don't, angel. You really, truly don't."

"Dante, you didn't hurt me. It made both of us feel good, and I liked it. So please stop over-thinking it."

He was quiet throughout the rest of the shower. Afterwards, he dried me so carefully and pulled me into his arms. "I can never do that to you again," he said, so quietly.

"I don't know why you're not hearing me when I tell you I liked it."

"That's not the point."

I sighed and wrapped my arms around him, holding on tight.

Chapter Nine

Dante had stayed with me all afternoon and evening after our shower, but I could tell he had a lot on his mind. We'd ordered dinner in and spent the evening Googling dog training videos on his phone. Finally when it was time for bed, he'd tucked me in and kissed me for a long time, then held me as I fell asleep.

I hadn't expected him to stay the night, of course, but I still missed him when I woke up alone the next morning. I got dressed, then donned the second pair of big falconry gloves that Dante had bought for me. I then tried to get Peaches leashed so I could take him for a walk.

The dog growled and raised his hackles when he saw me, but it was sort of half-hearted. He was obviously depressed and missing my mom. *Our mom*, I corrected myself with an eye roll. He still tried to bite the crap out of me when I got the leash on him and lifted him out of the pen, though.

Peaches was better when I got him outside, more interested in peeing on absolutely everything than in trying to kill me. We ended up taking a two-hour walk through Golden Gate Park, and he was good and tired by the time I got him home.

I put him back in the pen and got him some fresh water, then went to grab a can of his special gluten-free dog food. When I opened the cabinet where the dog's supplies were stored, I saw that Dante had purchased several cases of Peaches' expensive food. God, that man was thoughtful. I'd have to remember to thank him. I served Peaches his breakfast, and the dog only had the energy to sneer at me before tucking into his food.

Finally, I turned to the coffee maker and I saw the note that was stuck to the top of it. Three sentences. Twelve little words.

We can't do this anymore. I'm so sorry. I'll never forget you.

Dante had broken up with me.

I sank onto the kitchen floor and hugged my knees to my chest. "Oh God," I whispered.

I'd known him such a short time. But in just a few days, he'd become so incredibly important to me. His presence in my life had held the sadness at bay, made me forget all about the misery that my life had become. He'd made me feel cared for, at a time when I needed that so desperately. He'd been so good to me.

And now he was gone.

I sat there for a long time, trying to accept the fact that it was over. But somehow, I just couldn't.

Eventually, I realized what time it was. I pushed myself up off the floor and went to work in a daze. Clearly, my emotions were written all over my face, because as soon as

Jamie and Dmitri saw me they shepherded me into the office, matching looks of concern on their very different faces.

"What happened, Charlie?" Jamie asked, sitting beside me on the couch that was against one wall of his office.

"Dante broke up with me." Gradually, the sadness in me was seeping away, replaced with determination to do something about this, instead of just sitting back and taking it. "That's not okay with me."

"Did you tell him that?"

"Not yet. I've just spent the last hour being stunned, miserable and brokenhearted."

"Aw Charlie, I'm sorry," Dmitri said.

"I need to talk to him. I'm not just going to let him decide this arbitrarily. And I know why he's doing it. He's afraid of hurting me."

"He might have a point there," Jamie murmured, and I frowned at him.

I looked up at Dmitri and said, "I don't actually know where Dante lives. But you do, don't you?"

"Sure. He lives on Nob Hill. I used to live down the street from him," Dmitri said.

"I need to talk to him," I said, standing up. "Could you give me his address?"

Dmitri hesitated, then said, "Maybe you want to call, instead of going over there. Dante's getting ready to go out of the country on some family business, something came up unexpectedly this morning. I don't know what it is exactly, but I do know he's really agitated. He might not be very receptive to talking."

"How do you know that?" I asked him.

"I happened to call him about an hour ago with a question about one of our suppliers. I only got the sketchiest details, but I could tell something big is going down."

"I have to go see him, especially if he's about to leave the country."

"I wouldn't," Dmitri said.

"No, but I would. Can I please have his address, Dmitri?"

He sighed and wrote something on a slip of paper, which he handed to me. But then he added, "I'm telling you Charlie, if he's right in the middle of some sort of family crisis, you probably really shouldn't go over there."

"Okay, I've been forewarned. Thanks for the address," I said, and headed for the door. But then I remembered something, and turned back to Jamie. "Sorry about blowing off work today."

"It's okay. Cole's got it covered."

"I'm still sorry," I told him.

"It's fine," he said. "You've been going through a lot lately."

"Way too fucking much," I muttered as I left the office.

Chapter Ten

I totally ignored Dmitri's warning and drove straight to Dante's house. I found a parking spot down the block and walked up to what looked like a huge Italian villa, plunked down in the middle of San Francisco. It made me pause for a moment. I'd known Dante was wealthy, but this home was jaw-dropping. I shook off my astonishment and climbed the wide steps to the front door, perfectly in sync with someone else who'd walked up to the house from the opposite direction.

I turned to look at the cute blond twink climbing the steps with me, and he smiled sweetly and said, "Hiya."

"Hi."

He rang the bell when we reached the door, and as we waited, we both appraised one another. He was probably around nineteen and very thin, with big blue eyes and a mop of too-long blond curls. He wore several silver necklaces, a sheer, tight, black t-shirt that ended just above his navel and showcased a pair of silver nipple rings through the thin fabric, and very low-slung jeans with a wide belt. That was a whole lot of look for shortly past noon on a weekday, and I wondered if he'd somehow just come from a club.

When the door opened, the twink said cheerfully, "Hiya, Andre."

The big guy at the door frowned a little and said, "Austin." Then he looked at me and muttered to himself, "There's time for a three-way?" before stepping back and letting us in. I had absolutely no idea what he was talking about. Andre slunk off without further comment.

Austin started to go ahead of me into the massive foyer, and I asked him, "Hey, do you know where I can find Dante Dombruso?"

"New, huh?" the blond asked me with a smile that looked inexplicably sympathetic. He surprised me by taking my hand, and said, "I'll show you where his office is. I'm going there too. I'm Austin, but you probably already caught that."

"Charlie."

There was plenty of activity in the big house, with lots of people hurrying around. Austin wound his way through the hustle and bustle, taking a few turns and climbing a back staircase. He obviously knew his way around. I was glad he kept holding my hand, because if I ever lost him in this huge place, I'd probably end up wandering the halls for hours trying to find Dante. "You with one of the agencies, Charlie?" he asked.

I had no idea what that meant. "No."

"I'm with Prestige. If you ever get tired of independent work, look us up. Maybe if you came to work for them, they'd send us out on some tandem assignments." He winked and smiled at me. I was totally lost.

Eventually, we stopped in front of a big door. When my companion knocked, Dante called, "Come in," and Austin pushed the door open and towed me into the office with him. It took Dante a moment to glance up from the computer on his massive desk, and when he did, he looked absolutely stunned.

"Hiya, Mr. Dombruso," Austin said. "I found your one o'clock out on the steps. His name's Charlie. I'm sorry to barge in like this, but I have to get my equipment out of the playroom. I need it for an appointment this afternoon. I texted you a couple times this morning to ask if it was okay to swing by, but I guess you were busy. Mind if I grab my stuff?"

"Go ahead," Dante murmured. He hadn't taken his eyes off me.

Austin squeezed my hand and whispered, "Good luck," before letting go of me and leaving through a different door.

"What are you doing here, Charlie?" Dante asked quietly.

"I'm here to tell you I don't accept."

"Don't accept what?"

"Our breakup."

He knit his brows and said, "Wait, what?"

"You heard me."

"This isn't a subject that's up for debate, Charlie."

I crossed the room and leaned forward, my hands on his desk. "I know why you're doing this, Dante. You're freaked out because you think you hurt me, and—"

"I don't *think* I hurt you. I know." Dante stood up and crossed his arms over his chest. "We're not doing this anymore."

"I disagree."

"I don't have time for stubbornness right now, Charlie. I'm getting ready to head out of the country, and I have a lot to do before my plane leaves. There's nothing to discuss here anyway."

"You want this, Dante. Whatever it is that's happening between us, you want it. I know you do. I make you happy, just like you make me happy. You want this as much as I do."

That seemed to make him angry for some reason, and he said, "I'm just the rebound guy, remember? You're trying to get over Jamie, the love of your life, and I was just supposed to be a fling. You and I both know that. Only, you picked the wrong guy."

"You know as well as I do that it's becoming so much more than that."

His voice rose a little as he said, "Look, we had fun for a couple days. But didn't you hear me? I was *holding back* with you. What I did to you yesterday? That was *nothing*. It gets so much worse than that, Charlie."

"It doesn't matter."

"Sure it does."

I paused for a moment, then said, "You know what, Dante? I realized early on that there was only one way I could do this, only one way to be involved with you. I knew I couldn't date you a little. I couldn't trust you a little. I couldn't go to bed with you a little. If I was going to do this, if I was going to be involved with you, I had to be all in. I'm still absolutely prepared to do that, to do whatever it takes to be with you."

"But you're making a huge mistake. You have no idea who and what I really am."

"Of course I do."

"What are you basing that on? A couple dates where I was on my best behavior? That's not the real me."

"Sure it is."

Dante glared at me as he crossed his arms in front of him and pulled a pair of sleek, black handguns out of twin shoulder holsters. He slammed them down on the desk and growled, "Charlie Connolly, meet Dante Dombruso."

"Why…why are you armed?" I stammered, startled.

"Because I'm in the fucking *mafia*, Charlie."

"I already knew that."

"You don't really get it, though. I know you don't."

"I may not know the details of your job, but I know who you are, Dante."

"Do you know why I'm rushing off to Sicily on short notice?" he asked. "It's so I can catch a son of a bitch I've been after for years and fucking *kill him*."

"There's no way that's true."

Dante threw his head back and ran his hand up his forehead as he growled, "What is it going to take to get through to you?" Apparently an idea occurred to him all of a sudden. He came around the desk, grabbed my arm, and dragged me out the same doorway Austin had gone through.

As he towed me down a long hallway, I told him, "You don't have to drag me, Dante. I'm going willingly."

"Christ," he muttered.

We'd reached an open doorway at the end of the hall, and Dante pulled me inside as he announced, "This is my playroom, Charlie."

I blinked at the huge room. There were chains and ropes and whips and things I couldn't even identify. Austin straddled a bench in one corner of the space, sorting through a metal suitcase. He stopped what he was doing and watched us, his eyes wide.

"This is who I am," Dante said.

I turned to him and raised my chin as I met his gaze defiantly. "I hope you use each and every item in here on me."

"Fuck!" Dante yelled. "You just won't listen! I've got to leave for the airport in about five fucking minutes, and I am just not getting through to you!"

"I know who you are," I said. "I know there's this wild, dangerous side of you, and I know there's another side as well, one that's sweet and gentle and kind. And I want all of you, Dante, both sides, every part of it. *I want to be with you.*"

He sighed in exasperation. Then he pointed across the room. "See that boy over there, Charlie? That's Austin. He's a prostitute. I've been beating him and fucking him a couple times a week for almost a year. Austin understands what I am, even if you don't. Why don't you talk to him? You sure as hell won't listen to me, but maybe you'll listen to someone who's been where you're trying to go."

"You want me to think you're a bad person so I'll stay away from you, but I'm still not convinced. I'll *never* be convinced."

Dante seemed to have a flash of inspiration. He let go of me and crossed the room to the blond boy, saying, "Can you clear your schedule for the next forty-eight hours, Austin? I'll pay you triple your usual rate."

"Of course, Mr. Dombruso. The agency won't have a problem with that. You know you're their number one client." He pulled out his phone and fired off a quick text.

"Good. Thank you, Austin." Dante went to a cabinet against the wall, pulled open a drawer and rooted around in it. He then brought a set of manacles over to the skinny blond, and snapped a wide metal cuff on the boy's wrist as he said, "Your time starts now." He tugged on the chain, and Austin leapt up and followed him like a puppy.

He brought the guy right up to me, and then, before I realized what was happening, Dante grabbed my arm and snapped the other manacle onto my wrist. "Okay, that's weird," I said.

"Austin, your assignment is to explain to Charlie in excruciating detail exactly what I do to you, and exactly how much you hate every single minute of it."

"I don't hate it, Mr. Dombruso," he said with a reasonably convincing smile.

"Bullshit. Just be honest with Charlie. You know better than anyone what he'd be in for if he kept going out with me."

Austin looked at me with surprise and murmured, "You were going out?"

"Those cuffs don't open with a key," Dante continued. "There's a trick to them. It'll take you a day or two to figure it out, because it's really not obvious. That should give Austin enough time to talk your ear off."

I raised an eyebrow at him and said, "Seriously?"

"I'm sorry to do this to you, Charlie, but I need you to really, truly understand why we can't be together. I know it's really shitty and kind of insane to chain you to a rent boy and then flee the country. But, well, I'm doing it anyway. Don't let him follow me, Austin." Dante kissed my forehead and left the playroom quickly, and I actually burst out laughing.

I called after him, "Have a safe trip! See you when you get back!" I heard him swearing somewhere down the hall.

"You're not planning to run after him, are you? Because just so you know, I don't run," Austin told me.

"Nah, I'm not going to try to prevent him from catching his flight. I'm simply going to be waiting for him when he gets back."

"Well, good," Austin said. He tried to reach into his pocket for his vibrating phone, but was stopped short by the chain that linked us. I let him pull my hand over, and he took out his phone and read the screen, then said, "My employers approved the change of plans in my schedule, so I'm yours for the next two days." He grinned at me pleasantly.

"Sorry you got dragged into this," I said. "I'm sure it isn't your idea of a good time."

"On the contrary, I think this is hilarious. And of course, it's obviously not the first time someone's paid me to chain me up. Though being chained to another person is new." He thought about that for a beat, then amended, "Okay, that's not new. The fact that we're not fucking while we're chained together, *that's* new."

I raised an eyebrow at him, then said, "Let's go check the drawer these cuffs came from for a key, just in case Dante was lying and there really is an easy way to open them."

Chapter Eleven

I was still wearing manacles and my new blond accessory when I returned home an hour later. Austin remained amused as hell by the whole thing, which was good. It would have been no fun at all to be chained to a cranky rent boy for hours on end.

There had been no key, and on closer inspection of the cuffs, no lock either. I'd tried to figure them out and failed miserably. So until I either discovered the secret to opening them or located some sort of industrial grade metal saw, Austin and I were inseparable.

We were already adapting to our situation. Driving home had given us a crash course (thank God not literally) in teamwork. I'd driven with my right hand, my chained left arm crossed over my body, and Austin had shifted with his free left hand. That had been interesting, since he'd never actually driven stick. But he learned fast as I talked him through it.

Somehow we actually made it home that way, and as we stepped through the door of my apartment, Austin said cheerfully, "Any time you'd like me to begin my lecture on what a terrible person Dante Dombruso is, just let me know."

"We've got time, Austin. Pace yourself." We went through to the kitchen, and he stopped short when Peaches started growling at us from inside his pen.

"What the fuck is that?" he asked.

"That's Peaches."

Austin burst out laughing. "Of course it is."

"Want something to drink?" I asked as I pulled the refrigerator open and grabbed a soda, which I popped open with my thumb. Since Dante had fastened my left hand to Austin's right, I still had the use of my dominant hand. That was something, at least.

"I'm good. Thanks, though."

I regarded Peaches, who showed me his teeth when he saw me looking at him. "I need to take the dog for a walk. He probably needs to pee."

"Okay, let's go," Austin said agreeably.

"There's a problem. He won't let me pick him up. I need to put on those big leather gloves over there on the counter so he doesn't bite me, but I can't do that with my wrist chained."

He chuckled at that. "Wow, and you seemed so normal when I first met you."

"What does that mean?"

"You look like the archetypal all-American boy: clean-cut, wholesome." I noted that my rent boy had an impressive vocabulary, then chastised myself for having automatically assumed he wouldn't be that bright. He was saying, "But it turns out, you date mob bosses and keep rabid vermin as pets. You're a total freak."

I grinned at him. "Thanks."

"So, what happened between you two that led to this?" He jingled the chain that linked us.

"Dante got freaked out about hurting me and broke up with me, but I told him I didn't accept our breakup. Not when I know for a fact we both want to be together."

"How did he hurt you?"

"Um...." I blushed embarrassedly. But come on, I was talking to a prostitute. The guy had heard, and probably done, it all. I admitted honestly, "He spanked me so hard that he bruised me, and when he realized that, he got really upset and withdrawn. Right after that, he broke up with me."

"Now why the hell would that bother him?" Austin mused. "He bruises the hell out of me all the time, and doesn't bat an eye." But then a look of understanding appeared on his pretty face, and he said, "Oh."

"Oh what?"

"Oh, *he's in love with you.* That's why it upset him that he hurt you."

"He's not in love with me. We've only gone out a few times."

"So?"

"So people don't fall in love that fast."

"Not always. But it absolutely can happen." He looked surprisingly wistful as he said, "I'm not sure about love at first sight. But I wholeheartedly believe in love at first date. It can be real right from the start."

"Wow, you're a total romantic."

He grinned at me. "You say that like it's a bad thing."

"It's not. I was just thinking that it must make your job kind of difficult."

"Why? Because, as a romantic, I must forever be falling in love with my clients? Believe me, that's *not* a problem."

"How do you date in your line of work?"

"I don't."

"At all?"

"Why would I? I get more than enough sex on the job, and I'm not looking for a relationship, so what would be the point of dating?"

As I mulled that over, my phone rang in my pocket. When I fished it out, I didn't recognize the number on the screen. "Hello?"

"Is this Charlie Connolly?" a woman's voice asked.

"Yes."

"Charlie, this is Stana Dombruso. Dante's grandmother."

"Oh. Uh, hello, Mrs. Dombruso. How are you?"

"Fine, thanks."

"I'm glad to hear it. Um, out of curiosity, how did you get this number?"

"I copied it down from the call log on Dante's cellphone when he wasn't looking. Enough chit chat! You need to get your butt down to this hospital where they're keeping me, and I mean pronto."

My eyes went wide, and I stammered, "I'm sorry?"

"You heard me. I'm in Rosewood Memorial in Russian Hill, room one-oh-eight. Do you know where that is?"

"Yes ma'am."

"Get down here, Charlie," she demanded. And then she hung up on me.

I looked at Austin and asked, "Could you hear her on the phone?" He grinned and nodded. "What do you suppose she wants?"

"No clue, but we'd better hurry up and find out. You really shouldn't keep the woman who raised Dante Dombruso waiting, because I'm guessing she's probably a real badass."

"He was raised by his grandmother?" I asked.

"Yeah. Didn't you know that?"

"Nope."

Austin bit his lip and said, "There's a problem with going to meet Dante's grandmother."

"I know. Maybe if we drape a coat over our hands she won't notice that we're chained together. Because really, how do you explain this to someone's grandma?"

"A problem in addition to the totally obvious one."

"There's another problem, besides having to meet Dante's grandmother while in handcuffs?"

"I really can't go into a hospital dressed this way, Charlie, and I don't see how either of us can change our clothes, not with our wrists linked together." He looked self-conscious for the first time, and lowered his gaze.

I thought about our conundrum for a long moment. Then I peeled my new Forty Niners sweatshirt off my free arm and my torso, turning it inside out in the process. I rolled the remaining sleeve inside out as I pulled it down my chained arm and up onto his, then popped the sweatshirt over his head. He ran his free arm through the other sleeve and happily declared, "Genius!"

"It's inside out and absolutely enormous on you, but at least you're covered," I said, reaching over and rolling back the sleeve on his free arm for him. He was a very slender five-foot-nine, and the sweatshirt, which had already been oversized on my six-two frame, completely engulfed him, extending almost to his knees.

He reached around to the back of his neck, awkwardly unfastened his necklaces with one hand, and set them on the kitchen counter. "This is so much better. Maybe now hospital security won't immediately boot us out."

"I wish I could put on a nicer shirt," I said, gesturing at the plain navy blue t-shirt I'd had on under the sweatshirt. "Something with a collar. But oh well." As we headed for the door, I told the dog, "Sit tight, Peaches. We'll have to deal with you later." He didn't even raise his head from his paws as a low growl rumbled in his throat.

It didn't take long to awkwardly team-drive our way across town. We parked in the little lot behind Rosewood, a sleek, two-story private hospital and care facility, and signed in at the front desk, then found room one-oh-eight. When I knocked tentatively on the closed door, a voice called out, "That damn well better not be that son of a bitch Doctor Michelson again. Because I told that cocksucker I'm not taking any more fucking tests!"

I pressed my hand over my mouth to keep from laughing, and Austin chuckled and whispered, "Told you she'd be a badass."

I called out, "No, ma'am. It's Charlie Connolly."

"Well, for Christ's sake Charlie, come in! Why are you standing out in the hallway?"

"God help me," I whispered. I adjusted the fleece jacket that was draped over the manacles, and pushed the door open.

Mrs. Stana Dombruso was a tiny woman of about 80, propped up in a non-hospital-issue queen-size bed, surrounded by a sea of honey-colored linens. She wore a dark red velvet robe and matching velvet...well, turban, I guess. Mrs. Dombruso had put on lipstick in the same color, but hadn't been all that precise in her application, so her mouth now looked like it was on the diagonal. She grabbed a pair of enormous glasses from the nightstand and held them in front of her face, assessing us as we came into the room.

"Which one of you is Charlie?" she wanted to know.

"That's me, ma'am," I said, "and this is my friend Austin. I hope it's okay that I brought him."

"Of course it's okay. I get damn few visitors as it is. Like I'd say no to one more! Well, are you boys going to stand there, or are you going to pull up a chair and sit the hell down?"

Austin and I awkwardly took up positions in the two chairs at her bedside, while Mrs. Dombruso continued to study me like a bug under a microscope. Finally she set the glasses down and said, "You're a handsome boy, Charlie. I can see why my gay homosexual grandson is so smitten with you."

"I...I'm sorry?" I stammered. Austin made a little choking sound and coughed into his fist as he struggled to repress a laugh.

"You're the first boy he's ever talked about, Charlie. He thinks I have a problem that he's a gay homosexual. He used to bring these women home to meet me, pretty Sicilian girls with long hair and big boobs. I know he was doing that because he thought it was what I wanted. But that's not what I want, Charlie. You know what I *do* want?"

"No ma'am."

"I want that boy to be happy. The things he's endured in his life, Jesus, Mary and Joseph! It's been so much. He deserves some happiness now. Don't you agree?"

"Yes, ma'am."

"The first time I ever heard him say your name, I *knew*," she said. "I knew he'd finally found what he'd been searching for all those years. You're the one who can make him happy, Charlie." I smiled at that, and then she snapped, "So why the fuck did he break up with you?"

"How did you know he broke up with me?"

"Because when he came and saw me this morning, he was in a funk. At first, he wouldn't tell me what was wrong, but I finally got that much out of him. He wouldn't go into details, though. So what happened? Did you two have a fight? A lover's quarrel? Whatever it is, you can get past it. This is important, Charlie. Dante needs this. He needs you. You have to make him take you back."

"I'm trying, ma'am."

"Really?"

"Oh he is, Mrs. Dombruso," Austin chimed in. "Charlie went to see him earlier this afternoon and told him he refuses to let Dante break up with him."

Mrs. Dombruso was delighted at that, and clapped her thin, veined hands together. "That's what I want to hear! So you're already doing what I was going to tell you to do. You're a good boy, Charlie, and you'll be good for my gay

149

homosexual grandson, just as soon as you can convince him to stop being an idiot and get back together with you."

"Yes ma'am."

"I like almost everything about you, Charlie. You're such a handsome boy, and with good manners. The only thing I don't like is the fact that you're holding hands with this little blond cupcake right in front of me! Do you think I don't know what's going on under that coat? Was I born yesterday? Are you two-timing my grandson, Charlie?" she crunched up her face into a hard glare.

"Oh no, ma'am," Austin piped up. Just the faintest southern accent had crept into his speech. He yanked the jacket away, revealing our chained wrists, and said, "We're not holding hands. See?"

"So what is that? Some kinky sex thing?" Mrs. Dombruso demanded.

"No, ma'am," Austin told her. "Your grandson chained me to Charlie before he left for the airport. He wants Charlie to think he's a terrible person."

Mrs. Dombruso knit her brows at that. Then she said, "My grandson is an idiot. He's a good boy. But he's an idiot! Trying to make the only person he's ever fallen for think he's bad! Bah! I'd cuff his ear if he was here right now." I glanced at my companion. He was fighting to keep a straight face, his big blue eyes sparkling with delight.

"So where's your car, Charlie?" she asked.

"Around back in the parking lot. Why?"

"Because now that we've had our little talk, you're getting me the hell out of here." She threw back the covers and revealed that she was wearing a pair of black pants and low-heeled black pumps under her robe.

"Wait, what?" I stammered, jumping up from the chair and inadvertently dragging Austin up with me.

"You heard me. The doctors want to keep me in here another week, but no fucking way am I staying here that long! None of my family will listen to me, so you're getting me out of here, Charlie. You and Cupcake."

"But Mrs. Dombruso, you had a heart attack!" I exclaimed.

"It was a *mild* heart attack, and it was *days* ago. I'm fine, and I'm getting out of here with or without your help." She swung out of bed and stood directly in front of me, glaring up at me with her hands on her hips. Mrs. Dombruso was barely five feet tall (though the big velvet turban thing added some height) but she obviously thought she was pretty intimidating. "So what are you going to do? You gonna let a little old lady wander the streets of San Francisco all alone? Would you really do that to me, Charlie?"

I tried to dissuade her by saying, "Mrs. Dombruso, if I help you break out of the hospital, your grandson will never forgive me! You want us back together, right? So I probably shouldn't go and do something that's guaranteed to piss him off."

She considered that for a long moment as she turned from me and fished an enormous black handbag out from under the bed. "Well," she said, "you do have a point there." I visibly sagged with relief. Then she added, "But if I force you to help me escape, Dante can't possibly hold that against you."

"He'd never believe it! I'm twice as big as you," I pointed out. She was digging through her purse as I was talking. "I mean, how would he possibly believe that you forced me to…oh." The sight of the silver revolver in her hand shut me right up.

"Don't worry Charlie, I'm not going to shoot you. But now you can honestly tell my grandson that I forced you to help me at gunpoint. You had no choice but to agree! How on earth could he fault you for that?" She looked extremely pleased with herself.

"Mrs. Dombruso, can you please not point that thing at me?" I said as my throat went dry.

"I *have to* point it at you. Otherwise you won't have a truthful excuse for why you busted me out of here!" To Austin she said, "Here Cupcake, hold this so it doesn't look like I'm making a break for it." She shoved her big purse at him. He grinned and put it over his shoulder, then tossed the fleece jacket back over our linked hands.

"Stop helping," I whispered to him.

She shoved her huge glasses in place, which magnified her watery brown eyes and made her look like a cartoon owl. Then she climbed into a wheelchair that was sitting in a corner. Austin quickly draped a little blanket over her legs and she concealed the gun beneath it, but still held it pointed at me. "Let's roll," she said.

Austin pushed the chair and I walked beside it. "Slow and steady, boys," she told us. "Don't want to attract any attention here. Just an old lady going for a walk with her grandsons." She smiled pleasantly at every nurse we passed, most of whom gave her odd looks. What had Dante said about her terrorizing the entire nursing staff?

A little giggle slipped from Austin, and I gave him a dirty look. "What?" he said. "This is fun."

"That's because the gun's not pointed at you," I hissed.

"I cased the joint earlier," Mrs. Dombruso informed us. "There's a service entrance just past the cafeteria. We make it that far and we're golden." She waved happily to another nurse, with the hand that wasn't holding a firearm.

We somehow made it through the service entrance unnoticed. Damn it! I was hoping someone would stop us and question us, so Mrs. Dombruso would have to hand the gun over and return to her room.

Then again, maybe the woman was totally unhinged, and maybe if anyone had tried to stop us, it would have resulted

153

in bloodshed. In which case it was a good thing we made it to my truck without attracting any attention.

"Give me the keys, Charlie. I'm driving," she informed me as she hopped out of the wheelchair and swung open the driver's side door.

"Why wouldn't I be the one to drive?" I wanted to know.

"Because you've got a boy chained to your wrist!" she exclaimed.

"Do you even know how to drive a stick shift?"

"What, you think old people can't drive stick? That's just ageist. Give me the keys and get in the truck, Charlie, before we get caught," she said.

I handed over the keys with a deep sense of foreboding. Then I hurried around and got in the passenger side with Austin and slammed the door a couple times to get it to stay shut. There wasn't a whole lot of room in the cab, so he climbed on my lap. "Cozy," he said with a wink.

Mrs. Dombruso turned the key in the ignition, then shot out of the parking lot, grinding gears the whole way. She was holding the gun and trying to shift with the same hand, and finally she gave up and tossed the gun in Austin's lap. "Hold that for me, boys," she said.

I gasped in alarm at the thought of a loaded firearm being thrown around. But when I picked it up, I realized it wasn't a real gun at all. It was a plastic toy, painted to look like metal. There was a picture of Woody from Toy Story on the handle.

"Oh my God! It's fake!" I exclaimed, and Austin roared with laughter.

Mrs. Dombruso said, "Of course it's fake! What, you think they'd let me bring a real gun into a hospital?"

"Why do you have a fake gun?" I wanted to know.

"Because my great grandson, Mikey Junior, left it behind when he and his family visited me yesterday. Who knew it would come in so handy?"

A few minutes later, after a fairly death-defying drive through town, we pulled up to the very grand, very historic Mark Hopkins Hotel. Mrs. Dombruso apparently didn't believe in turn signals, or slowing down to less than fifty, ever, not even on crowded city streets.

"What are we doing here?" I asked.

"I'm checking in. Not like I can go home," Dante's grandmother said. "My family would find me there and drag me right back to that goddamn hospital."

Austin turned to me with wide eyes. "Can we have a drink at the Top of the Mark while we're here? Pretty please?"

"Are you even old enough to drink?"

"I'm old enough for a bottled water with a panoramic view of San Francisco."

"How old are you, anyway?" I asked as we climbed out of the cab and Mrs. Dombruso handed over the keys to a valet.

"Twenty."

"Really?"

"Want to card me?" he asked with a grin.

Mrs. Dombruso plucked off her glasses and shucked her robe, draping it over her arm along with her purse. She was wearing a sparkly black suit underneath. She kept the velvet headpiece on though, and held her head high as she strolled regally into the Mark Hopkins.

Austin slipped his hand into mine beneath the draped jacket as we waited for Mrs. Dombruso to check in. He'd become subdued when we entered the lobby and stood close to me, his head down. "You okay?" I asked.

"Any minute someone's gonna walk up to us and ask us what we're doing here," he said quietly, darting looks around the lobby from under his thick, dark lashes.

"If they do, I'll tell them we're here with the Queen of Sheba," I said, tilting my head toward Mrs. Dombruso with a little grin.

He smiled at that and looked up at me. "This place intimidates the hell out of me. I still want to see the Top of the Mark, though. I've always wanted to see it."

"Okay, we'll do that."

Mrs. Dombruso had procured a huge, lovely suite with stunning views of the city and the bay beyond. Once she was settled, I told her, "We'll just go ahead and get out of your way. I wanted to make sure you got in safely, and now you have. Call me if you need anything." I fully intended to rat her out to her family the moment I got out of there.

"Oh no," she said. "You're not running away so quickly. We're going to have drinks and dinner together at the Top of the Mark. I heard the little pretty one saying he wanted to see it, and I want to get to know the handsome boy that has my Dante smitten."

Oh man.

Her cellphone rang and she pulled it out of her purse and looked at the screen, then rolled her eyes and put it on the writing desk. It stopped ringing after a moment. Then mine started.

I pulled it out of my pocket. There was an unfamiliar number on the screen, but I could guess who it was. I hit speaker and answered with, "Hi Dante. Where are you?"

"On a plane bound for Sicily. Charlie, did you bust my grandmother out of the hospital?" The connection wasn't so great. He sounded a bit tinny, and there was a constant hum in the background. But I could still hear the exasperation in his voice.

"I...."

"Did you?"

"No. Not...technically."

"What does that mean?"

"I mean, technically, I was a hostage."

"What?"

"She had me at gunpoint," I explained.

"Where did my grandmother get a gun?" Dante demanded.

"It turned out to be a toy gun," Austin chimed in. "Mikey Junior's, apparently. How's your flight so far, Mr. Dombruso? Are you calling from one of those phones in the back of the seats?"

"It looked real," I said in my defense.

"Mikey Junior's? Do you mean his Toy Story cowboy gun?"

"Yeah, that one," I confirmed.

"Are you *serious*?"

Mrs. Dombruso grabbed the phone from me and said, "Aw, quit busting the boy's balls, Dante! He didn't have a choice. He tried to talk me out of leaving the hospital, but I was a desperate woman. So I did the only thing I could do. I took him hostage!" She sat down in a big upholstered chair and put her feet up, grinning smugly.

"With a plastic gun," Dante said.

"What, you would prefer that I pointed a real gun at your love muffin?"

"And he didn't know the difference?" Dante asked incredulously.

"Charlie's a nice boy. So he doesn't know a real gun from a fake one. So sue him."

Dante changed the subject and said, "You need to go back to the hospital, Nana."

"Ain't happening."

"You had a *heart attack*. You need to go back."

"I'm fine."

"Where are you now? Are you at home?" he asked her.

"No. I'm at a secret location."

"Are you at the Mark Hopkins again?"

She threw up her hands. But then she said levelly, "Of course not. That'd be the first place you'd look."

"This isn't safe, Nana. You need to be under a doctor's care."

"I know, and that's why Doctor Jensen is coming to check up on me here at my secret location daily, beginning tomorrow. So are a team of home healthcare nurses. I got it all arranged. I'm not stupid," she told him.

"It's still not as good as a hospital."

"Tough shit," she said.

Dante sighed dramatically. After a pause he asked, "What was Charlie doing at the hospital?"

"I called him and told him to come see me."

"How did you call him? I didn't give you his number."

"I got it from your call log when I told you I wanted to borrow your phone to send a text," she explained. "I mean seriously, who the hell am I going to be texting? Maury

Baumgartner? Gloria Mazetti? My friends are older than dirt, Dante. They don't *text*. You're so gullible."

"Christ," Dante muttered.

"Also," she continued, "what kind of idiot chains the boy he's smitten with to a blond hottie? I mean, who does that? What do you want, for these two to fall in love while they're forced to spend all this time together and leave you out in the cold? What were you thinking?"

Dante sighed again, then said, "Look Nana, I gotta go. Do you swear the doctor and some nurses are going to be coming and checking on you?"

"I swear it on your grandfather's grave."

"Grandpa isn't dead, Nana. He's living in Florida with a thirty-six-year-old waitress named Prudence."

She spit on the floor and yelled, "He's dead to me!"

"I'm calling Doctor Jensen's office as soon as we hang up. I'm verifying that he's really coming to check on you."

"You're so suspicious."

"I love you, Nana. Please take care of yourself," he said.

"I love you too, Sugar. Be safe."

"I will," Dante said, and he disconnected the call.

"Mrs. Dombruso," I asked, "why is Dante on his way to Sicily?"

"Because he got a good lead as to the whereabouts of that bastard Sal Natori," she told me. "And maybe, just maybe, he'll finally have a chance to kill that son of a bitch."

"Wait...Dante is flying halfway around the world *to kill someone*?"

"Didn't he tell you?" Mrs. Dombruso asked as she handed my phone to me.

"He did, actually. I didn't believe him." I stared at her incredulously. "And...you're okay with this?"

"Well, I'm worried about Dante, of course. Natori's a very dangerous man. But this needs to be done. My grandson will never rest until he puts Sal Natori in the ground."

"Dante's in danger?"

"Yeah."

I sank onto a corner of the bed and murmured, "This conversation has just gotten absolutely surreal." With his free hand, Austin rubbed my back comfortingly.

Mrs. Dombruso got to her feet and said, "You look like you could use a drink, Charlie. Come on, let's go upstairs and show this little cutie the Top of the Mark." She turned and bustled from the suite.

We were quite the ragtag group, me in my t-shirt and jeans with a jacket draped over the cuffs on my wrist, Austin in his big inside-out sweatshirt, and Mrs. Dombruso in her huge velvet head wrap and crooked lipstick. But the maître d' greeted her warmly by name, and we were immediately ushered to a table at one of the windows. We arranged ourselves so Austin was beside the glass, and he stared out at the sprawling cityscape with childlike wonder.

Mrs. Dombruso insisted on treating, and soon the table was loaded up with every appetizer on the menu. I was too dazed to eat, and Austin claimed he wasn't hungry, but Mrs. Dombruso tucked in eagerly. "That hospital food, ugh! I wouldn't give it to a dog!" she exclaimed.

I took a sip of the beer she'd bought me, then asked, "Ma'am, could you please tell me what exactly Dante's doing? I mean, I know you said he's going to kill someone. But why? And...does he do that a lot?" The whole mafia thing had suddenly gone from abstract concept to all too real.

"What, kill people? Of course not," she said. "Dante, he's more of what you'd call an executive. He runs a business. Granted, it's an *illegal* business. But a business nonetheless."

"Then what's he doing now?"

Mrs. Dombruso dabbed her mouth with a thick cloth napkin and said, "In order to answer that question, I gotta tell you a story, Charlie. And it's a terrible story. You wanna hear it?"

"Yes please."

She paused for a long moment, and turned her head to look out the window. Finally she said, "You know the business my family is in. Well, we've been in that business for eight generations. Every generation has had its natural leaders, like Dante, and like his father before him. Trouble is, leaders always have the biggest targets on their backs.

"My son Paulie, Dante's father, he made a lot of enemies. It happens in this line of work. One of these enemies, a man by the name of Sal Natori, decided to make it personal. He went after my son not on the streets, but in his home, at night, while Paulie and his family were sleeping. He took several men with him and broke in and shot my son and his wife right in their bed. And…" her voice wavered and she made the sign of the cross as she said, "and then they went after the children. They got to little Sophie's bedroom first and put a bullet in that beautiful, precious baby girl. Then they went down the hall to the boys' room."

Her hands and her voice shook as she continued, still staring off into the distance, "Dante, he must have heard something. I don't know what. The men were using silencers. But when they got to the boys' room, Dante was ready for them. He had a gun pointed at the men. He'd found one of his father's big hunting rifles, I don't even know how he could lift it. And he'd gone to his little brothers' room to protect them. He held off the men while Mikey, Johnnie and Vincent climbed out the window. They were just three, four and five, poor little angels. Dante had them run to the neighbors for help, it's the only reason they survived."

She dabbed her eyes with her napkin. "Little Dante, he shot one of those men, killed him dead as he lunged for the escaping boys. But another man caught Dante and made him drop the rifle. They were gonna kill my grandson, but they decided to smack him around first, make him pay for taking out one of their own."

"Oh God," I whispered.

"Fortunately, the shotgun blast had awakened a couple of Paulie's men who were staying up in the converted attic, and they got downstairs in time to save Dante." Her watery eyes met mine as she said quietly, "He was only seven years old, Charlie. He was a baby. Those men, they scarred him for life. They took his parents and sister. And now, twenty-two years later, he's closing in on that animal. This time, he's got a solid lead. He may finally get to avenge the death of his family."

"But what if Natori kills Dante?" I said softly. Austin laced his hand with mine and gave it a reassuring squeeze.

"That's a chance my grandson is willing to take. Dante feels it's his duty to go after Natori and avenge his family. If he's successful this time, if he kills that piece of shit, then maybe it'll finally bring Dante some peace. He's still tormented by the death of his parents and sister. He can't sleep to this day. Maybe once Natori's dead, Dante will finally have some of that, you know. Closure."

"Dante's not doing this alone, is he? Please tell me he's not going after Natori by himself."

"No way. He's got a team of his best men with him. He's not taking unnecessary chances with his safety."

I whispered, "Oh God, if Dante is killed…."

"You can't think like that, Charlie. You gotta trust in the fact that he's strong and capable, and he's going to do everything in his power to come back to you."

"He has to," I said quietly.

Chapter Twelve

I was mentally drained by the time I got back to my apartment with Austin in tow, but I still had to deal with Peaches. Working together with one big glove on each of our free hands, Austin and I managed to get the smelly little beast out of the pen and leashed. We then took him for a long walk before bringing him back home and feeding him his dinner.

I didn't have the heart to put him back in the pen after that, which meant that Austin and I had to hide in the bedroom with the door shut to keep from getting chewed on. I fell across my mattress and Austin sat cross-legged beside me as I asked, "Would you take a look at the manacles, see if maybe you can figure out how to open them?"

"Sure."

He rested my chained hand on his thigh, and I felt his delicate touch on my skin as he circled the edge of the wide metal cuff, feeling for hidden levers or springs. After just a couple minutes of that, he stopped his exploration and patted the back of my bound hand with his free one.

"Giving up already?" I murmured.

"It's an incredibly complex design. More art than S & M, really. I wonder where Mr. Dombruso got these."

I felt him pulling the back of my t-shirt out of my jeans, and turned my head to look at him. "What're you doing?"

"I want to see how bad your bruises are," he said quietly, and carefully tugged the waistband of my jeans down a few inches.

"Can you see them?"

"Yup. You'd feel a lot better if you soaked in a hot bath," he said, releasing my waistband. "It would disperse the bruises more quickly, too. Do you have a tub?"

"Yeah, there's a tub-shower combo. I'm not really a bath kind of guy, though."

"You might want to learn to be."

I rolled onto my side and looked at Austin. "What do you mean?"

"I mean," he said matter-of-factly, "that if you do get back together with Mr. Dombruso, you'll need to learn ways to recover from the things he's going to do to you. A hot bath is a good basic starting point."

I stared at him for a long moment as he held my gaze steadily. Finally, I said, "Yeah, okay, I think I will go and soak. Which of course means you get to hang out in the bathroom with me."

"Not a problem."

I plugged the tub and started the water running, then stripped down to my boxer briefs. I couldn't take my t-shirt off with the cuffs, so I asked, "Would you hold this for me?" When he nodded, I pulled it off my free arm and my torso and rolled the shirt up onto his arm so it would stay out of the water.

Then I said embarrassedly, "Um, I need to pee." Austin turned his back to me and stepped as far away as possible to give me the illusion of privacy, and I did what I had to do with one hand.

When I climbed into the water, Austin glanced at me and grinned. "You're still wearing your underwear."

"In retrospect, I suppose a bathing suit would have made more sense."

He sat on the edge of the tub and said, "You know, you don't have anything that I haven't seen before."

"We're being forced to live in awfully close proximity here. I figure maintaining a sense of privacy will make this a little more comfortable for both of us."

I spent several minutes examining the metal cuffs as I steeped in the hot water. They were really intricate, several narrower bands of metal interwoven into a wider cuff. I didn't have a clue how they'd possibly open. Finally I gave up, leaned back in the tub, and said, "So, why don't you go ahead and deliver your lecture? Get it over with. Tell me what a terrible person Dante is, and why I shouldn't be with him."

"Before that, I need to ask you one question. Please answer honestly."

"Alright."

He looked me in the eye as he asked, "Did you like it when Mr. Dombruso spanked you?"

I blushed deeply, but went with total honesty. "It was wonderful. I don't think I've ever been that aroused. I not only absolutely enjoyed it, I felt like I *needed* it."

A little half-smile tugged at the corner of Austin's full lips, and he said, "I was hoping you'd say that. If you'd hated every minute of it and were enduring it just for his sake, then I would have felt obligated to try to steer you away from him."

"But now you don't?"

"The thing is, I like Mr. Dombruso. He doesn't think I do. A lot of clients treat me like trash, like I'm worthless. But he's always treated me with respect. I actually think he's a good man."

"Why does he think you hate him?"

Austin grinned and said, "That's probably because I would spend the entire time he was whipping me cussing him out. That was another good thing about him, he really didn't seem to mind being called every name in the book."

"Really?"

"Well then again, he probably did mind. But he let me do it anyway. He knew that was my coping mechanism, and he let me do it because it helped me get through it." Austin shifted on the rim of the tub, crossing his legs and taking my hand between both of his so he could rest it on his lap.

"Is it weird that I liked it when he spanked me?" I knew how ridiculously naïve that sounded, but I just had to know if I was a total freak of nature.

"Not at all. See, with me, I'm not naturally submissive, and that's why I hated it so much. Actually, I'm not even naturally a bottom. I just take those roles when my job requires it. But there's nothing wrong with the fact that it gets you off. Plus, it means that you and Mr. Dombruso are really sexually compatible."

"Did, um…did he beat you every time?" The questions were super embarrassing, but there was so much I wanted to know.

"Without fail. Every session began with him tying me down. Next he whipped me or spanked me until he was aroused, and then he fucked me, hard. The only variations were how he chose to tie me down, and what implement he used to do the whipping. As you saw in the playroom, there was a lot to choose from."

"I didn't even know what most of that stuff was."

"Everything in that room serves one of two functions: either it's for tying someone up, or it's for beating them. Because that's what gets him off, plain and simple."

"I'm really inexperienced when it comes to this stuff, obviously," I admitted. "I only had one boyfriend before Dante, and we actually never went farther than oral sex. I kind of feel incredibly clueless about…well, pretty much everything."

"Anything you want to know, I'll tell you."

"Thank you. I really appreciate you being so open with me."

"You didn't ask, but I'm going to tell you something else, because you might worry about it down the road: he used a condom with me one hundred percent of the time. For the record," he added, "I don't have any STDs. I don't know how the hell that's possible, given all the shit that's been done to me. But anyway, just so you know, he always played safe."

"Good to know."

"You also didn't ask this question," Austin said with a smile. "But he hasn't fucked me since he met you. Mr. Dombruso actually texted me the night he met you in a bar, because we had an appointment that night. He cancelled on short notice, and hasn't rescheduled since then. You know, just in case you were wondering."

*****

When we got ready for bed that night, Austin traded his tight jeans for a pair of my sweats, which were ridiculously big on him. He cinched them up as much as he could with the drawstring, and between that and the toothbrush I gave him

171

out of the twin pack I'd bought at the dollar store, we made do pretty well.

Finally, I shut off the lights and we got under the covers. We were about two feet apart and facing each other, our bound hands at shoulder height between us. Austin watched me for a while, his eyes full of some sort of emotion. Then he said quietly, "You know you can fuck me if you want, I'm bought and paid for. You can do anything you want to me. I'm a full-service whore."

I reached up with my free hand and gently brushed the blond curls back from his face. "You really don't want me to do that. Why would you bring it up?"

He shrugged, breaking eye contact. "You didn't ask to be stuck with me, and it has to be wearing on you, being forced to spend all this time with a prostitute. So I thought…I don't know. Maybe if I could make you feel good, this would seem like less of an ordeal to you."

"You know, if I was stuck with anyone else, this probably *would* seem like an ordeal. But you're incredibly easy to get along with, Austin. You're a nice person, and I actually really like spending time with you."

He met my gaze. "You do?" I nodded and he smiled shyly. "I like you, Charlie. I'm kind of glad we're stuck with each other."

Chapter Thirteen

The next morning when I awoke, I was lying flat on my back on my side of the bed, and Austin was wound around me like a cute, blond boa constrictor. He was partially on top of me, his head on my chest, his thin arm holding me tightly, straddling one of my legs with both of his and snoring softly. When I shifted slightly he woke with a start, and realizing he'd intertwined himself with me, got off me quickly with a mumbled, "Sorry."

We got up and dressed, and I placed a quick call to the hotel and spoke to Dante's grandmother, who assured me she was fine. Then Austin and I teamed up to wrestle Peaches onto his leash and took him for a walk. When we got back to the apartment, I had some cereal while Austin again claimed not to be hungry. I was beginning to wonder if he ever actually ate.

As I was cleaning up after breakfast, Austin chewed his thumbnail and glanced at me, then quickly looked at the floor. "Go ahead and ask me," I said.

"Man. Am I that obvious?"

"Yup. Is there something you need to do today?"

"I mean, I'm on the clock, so it doesn't really matter."

"I was sprung on you with absolutely no notice, Austin, so if you have something you need to do today, please tell me and we'll make it work."

"Don't worry, it's not a sex thing," he said.

"That didn't even cross my mind."

"Well, I actually have a class at ten a.m. I'd blow it off, except that I have an assignment that's due today, and I don't want to get marked down."

"That's not a problem. How long's the class?"

"Ninety minutes. My day's wide open after that. Beforehand though, I need to swing past my apartment to change and pick up a couple things."

"Sure, and if it's okay with you, I'd like to try going to work after class. Waiting tables while chained to another person might be problematic, but I already blew off yesterday, and I don't want my ex to think I'm making a habit of it."

"You work for your ex?"

"Yup."

"How is that?"

"Awkward," I said, pulling my phone from the pocket of my jeans.

Jamie answered on the second ring with, "How are you, Charlie?"

"I'm alright."

"How did it go with Dante yesterday?"

I glanced at the cuff on my wrist. "Not quite as expected, but not bad, I suppose. So hey, I'm sorry to be such a flake, but I'm going to be a little late today."

"That's fine. Cole can hold down the fort until you get here."

I left out the part about coming to work attached to another person. Maybe there was a chance I'd get the manacles open before the start of my shift. Then I could skip having to explain all of this to Jamie.

*****

Austin and I decided to take public transit, since he said parking was nonexistent both in his neighborhood and at school. When we got off the bus downtown, I was a little surprised. I'd forgotten that parts of San Francisco could be quite so bad.

Litter and graffiti punctuated the landscape. Even this early in the morning, dead-eyed prostitutes clustered in doorways, skimpy outfits doing nothing to protect them from the cold September day. Homeless people stood and sat and laid on the sidewalk. A couple rough-looking men were having a heated argument, which soon erupted into a fight. It didn't last long though, and after taking a couple brutal hits, one of the men staggered away in defeat.

I took a look at my companion as he led the way into his building. His head was down, shoulders slouched, like he was trying to remain unnoticed. How did a boy like Austin survive in a place like this? It would be so easy for people to hurt him, or rob him, or take advantage of him. Even something as simple as coming and going from his apartment each day must be a lesson in survival.

We entered the lobby of the building. There seemed to be no electricity, so the lobby was only lit by the weak sunlight that filtered through a couple filthy windows. A man in a suit was having sex with a woman at the foot of the stairs. She was obviously a prostitute, her short skirt pushed up over her hips as he bent her over. Austin took my hand and led me around the couple and up the steps. He glanced over his shoulder at me as he said, "Sorry about that. The old manager used to keep people from working in the lobby. The new guy doesn't really seem to give a shit about anything."

We climbed up four flights of stairs before he led me, still holding my hand, down a long, dark hallway littered with garbage and reeking of urine. Behind one of the doors, a loud argument was taking place. A big guy was weaving down the hall toward us, obviously either drunk or on drugs, muttering incoherently. When the man got close to us, my companion gently pushed me against the wall and put himself between the drunk and me. I realized he was protecting me. The man passed without incident, and Austin picked up my hand again and led me to a doorway almost at the end of the hall.

He pulled a key out of the pocket of his jeans and unlocked the door, and I followed him inside. The room was tiny but clean, the little twin bed neatly made. A clothesline stretched across one end of the space, and a toilet and sink were in the corner. A small bouquet of daisies in a glass soda bottle sat on the sill of the barred window, which struck me as incredibly touching.

The room was fairly dark and cold, and when I flipped the light switch, the bare bulb hanging from the ceiling did nothing. "Power's been out for a few days," he said as he checked the clothes on the line, squeezing the fabric to see if it was dry and then pulling down a pair of jeans and some briefs. "The wiring in this place is kind of iffy, but they always get it working again sooner or later."

I turned away to give him some privacy as he kicked off his sneakers and shimmied out of his tight low-rise jeans, then managed to get his underwear and the new slightly baggy jeans on mostly with one hand. When I turned back around to him, he was slipping his feet into a pair of beat-up Converse.

"Do you go to S.F. State?" I asked as he towed me around the room, gathering a backpack and something that looked like a tackle box.

"No, I go to Sutherlin."

"The private art college?"

"That's where all the money goes that I earn by turning tricks, in case you're wondering why I live in such a shit hole." Austin fished around in his backpack and took out a little sealed package of square, bright orange crackers sandwiched together with peanut butter. He held the package out to me and offered me some, and when I declined he quickly ate all of them. He was obviously incredibly hungry.

"So, you do eat. I was beginning to wonder."

I'd said that jokingly, but his expression was serious as he said, "I, um, I have a lot of issues when it comes to food. This is the only thing I eat, actually." Before I could ask questions, he hoisted the backpack onto his shoulder and said, "We'd better get going. I don't want to be late."

I carried the tackle box for him, and we left the hell of his building and emerged back out onto the hell of the sidewalk. He visibly relaxed only when he was out of his neighborhood.

We rode another bus across town, and then I watched as another transformation came over Austin. As we walked onto Sutherlin's campus, his whole demeanor changed. He seemed younger, almost buoyant, as his pace increased and his body realigned subtly. He stood up straighter, with his shoulders back, as if he was in his element. As if he was home.

"Shouldn't we be covering up these handcuffs?" I asked. We'd employed the fleece jacket method on public transit, but he was holding the jacket in his hand now and making no effort to disguise the fact that we were chained together.

He glanced at me with a sparkle in his eye. "This is art school, Charlie. Almost no one's going to bat an eye at something like this. If they do, we can just claim it's performance art or something. Let me do the talking."

"Fine by me."

When we reached the door of a large studio, he paused and looked up at me. "One thing. Call me Christopher Robin."

"Why?"

"Because that's my real name," he said with a little grin, and pushed the door open.

Several students greeted him as we cut through the large, sunny space to an easel on the far side of the room. "Hey C.R.," a Goth girl called out. A dozen piercings sparkled from her lips, nose, and eyebrows. "What's with the cute brunet?"

Most of the students turned toward us to hear the answer. Austin, or no, Christopher Robin, replied, "This is my friend Charlie. He's a student at S.F. State, and he's doing a project for his psychology class. It's about empathy, about polar opposites, a jock and an art student, learning to see the world through each other's eyes. We're spending forty-eight hours chained together for his experiment."

He was one smooth liar, he hadn't missed a beat. Every single person in the room bought that explanation, a couple of them saying, "Oh," and, "That's cool."

A woman in a paint-covered smock came up to us. She was slightly older than the rest, and she asked, "Are you going to be able to paint like that, Christopher Robin?" I realized she must be his teacher.

"I think so, Sandra. Charlie will need to cooperate with me in order for this to be successful, so it'll be an excellent lesson in teamwork." She nodded and crossed the room to speak to another student.

He dragged a stool over for me and placed it beside his, and as he pulled things out of the tackle box I whispered with a grin, "Thanks for portraying me as a dumb jock."

"I never said dumb, and I think they bought the school project excuse."

"Of course they did. It's almost scary what a good liar you are."

"I lie for a living," he whispered back. "I mean, think about it. How many disgusting old men have I had to lie to over the years, convincing them they were sexy and desirable? Convincing them I didn't hate every single thing they were doing to me?"

"That's sad."

"That's life," he shrugged.

I whispered as quietly as I could, "Why do you work as a prostitute, Austin?" I corrected myself and amended, "I mean, Christopher Robin?"

"Long story. Someday, maybe I'll regale you with the tragic tale of Christopher Robin Andrews, hooker and lost boy. But today," he said with a grin as he set up his art supplies, "is not that day."

He settled down on his stool as a young woman in a robe took the small stage in the center of the room, arranging herself carefully on the wooden chair. I whispered, "Oh no, don't tell me this is a—" she dropped the robe, exposing every inch of her body, and I blushed furiously as I said, "life drawing class." I quickly looked away from the model.

"Close. Life painting." Christopher Robin carefully removed a white drape from the canvas on his easel, and I actually gasped. The painting was nearly complete, and it was absolutely stunning. It was photo-realistic, rendered in amazing detail. Even a dolt like me who knew absolutely nothing about art knew that was something absolutely extraordinary. I looked at the model again, and looked at the painting. I saw how he'd perfectly captured the woman's expression, including a bit of melancholy that I hadn't seen in her at first.

"Holy shit, Chris," I murmured.

"I don't go by Chris, just FYI. You can call me Christopher, if my full name is just too much of a mouthful." He grinned at me and added, "Once we leave here and return to your world, you can go back to calling me Austin if you want."

He turned his attention to painting, and since he was right-handed (the hand that was chained to me) I tried my damnedest to concentrate and follow his movements as I held onto his arm. I also tried to make sure I didn't clumsily jar him or hinder what he was doing in any way.

"Don't try to anticipate where I'm going to move my hand," he said gently at one point. "Just relax your arm, let me guide you."

"I'm worried that my arm's too heavy. I was trying to lighten the weight of it on you."

He smiled at me. "I know, Charlie, and thank you. I'm a lot stronger than I look, though, so you can go ahead and relax." I tried to do that.

When the class ended an hour and a half later, the teacher came up to us and took a look at Christopher's canvas. She was positively beaming. To me she said, "This boy is my star pupil. I'd like to pretend I taught him everything he knows, but that's not true at all. He's a prodigy. Did you know your friend can do this?"

"I had no idea. He's a very surprising person." Wasn't that the truth!

After he packed up his supplies, Christopher picked up his canvas carefully and took it over to a long, thin shelf along one wall, where all the students were lining up their paintings. "This assignment's done," he explained. "We're turning them in. That's why I didn't want to miss school today."

I took a look at the other paintings. All of them were good, some of them wonderful. But my companion's was from a different universe. It was so much better than the rest that it looked like it had been plucked from a museum. Apparently, I wasn't the only one who thought so. As soon as his painting went up, a crowd gathered. "Holy shit," one guy said, "why do I even bother painting?"

"Damn, C.R., you never cease to amaze," the Goth girl from earlier said.

"Christopher Robin's gonna go on to rule the art world," a skinny kid with wild, crayon red hair told me with a big smile. "And all of us are gonna get to say 'I knew him back at the beginning.' I just hope that in the art school scenes when they make the movie of his life, I'm played by someone hot."

"You're gonna be played by a mop dipped in red paint," someone told him, and everyone laughed.

"But seriously, Christopher Robin," a petite blonde girl said, "This is mind-blowing."

My companion looked embarrassed by all of the attention and blushed shyly. "You guys are too sweet," he murmured. "Well, we gotta run, Charlie has to get to work. See you next week." He grabbed his stuff, and we took off to a chorus of goodbyes.

*****

We came in through the front door when we finally arrived at Nolan's an hour into my shift. It was actually fairly busy. I apologized to Cole as we hurried past, and he raised an eyebrow at us.

At my locker, my companion put away his backpack and art supplies as I picked up a clean work t-shirt from the shelf and said, "Ok, so how am I going to put this on?"

"You could split it down the seam under your chained arm," he suggested. "Then I could stitch it back up for you."

"That'd take too long."

Jamie came out of the kitchen and said, "Hey Charlie. Who's your friend?"

I turned to the boy in question and asked, "Are you Austin now, or are you Christopher Robin?"

He smiled up at me and said, "That's your call."

"Jamie, this is Christopher Robin Andrews. Christopher, this is Jamie Nolan. It's his bar."

"Ah. So you must be the ex," Christopher said, and stuck out his hand to shake Jamie's. His *right* hand, the one that was attached to me.

Jamie's eyes went wide, but he shook his hand and said politely, "It's nice to meet you." Then he looked at me and asked, "Is there a reason you two are chained together?"

"It's a kinky sex thing," I told him. Jamie already disliked Dante. I wasn't going to give him fuel for his argument that the guy was bad for me.

184

Christopher chuckled at that, and Jamie raised an eyebrow at me. "Oh yeah, you're totally into kinky sex, Charlie. So what's the real reason? No, never mind, tell me later. Cole needs help out there. Just tell me you'll unchain yourself long enough to work your shift."

"No can do. There's no key. But I can work like this, with the exception of being able to pull a work shirt on over the chains."

Jamie was fighting the urge to roll his eyes, I could tell. But he said, "Go ahead and work without it," and went back into the kitchen.

I tied my black apron around my hips, went out into the dining room and got busy, refilling drinks and clearing a couple plates. I went to refill a beer and found Dmitri behind the bar. It somehow always seemed really incongruous to see him doing something as mundane as working. At least to me. A man that beautiful seemed like he should be lounging on a Hollywood movie set or something, not serving drinks.

"Hi Charlie. Hi Austin," he said cheerfully. His cornflower blue eyes were sparkling with amusement.

"Hi Mr. Teplov," my companion said with a smile.

"It's just Dmitri," my ex's husband corrected. Then he asked me, "Out of curiosity Charlie, why are you chained to a prostitute?"

"How do you know he's a prostitute?"

"Dante introduced us when I ran into Austin at his house." I was a little surprised that Dante was so forthcoming about his sex life. Then I remembered how the guy at the door when I'd gone to see Dante had let Christopher in without question. In a delayed light bulb moment, I realized the guy had thought I was a prostitute as well, there to do a three-way with Christopher and Dante. Man, a lot of people were up in Dante's business.

"Um, the cuffs are a long story. I have to give Cole a hand, so I'll tell you later."

"I can't wait to hear it," Dmitri said with a big smile, dimples out in full force.

A table was seated in my section, and when we went up to them and they gave us a funny look, Christopher told the two businessmen, "We're on a game show. If we can survive like this for a week without killing each other, we win a cash prize." They wished us luck.

At the next table, he told a group of college students with long hair and political t-shirts, "We're doing a school paper on abuses in the criminal justice system, and are learning how a man's dignity is stripped from him when he's forced to wear handcuffs."

"Right on, man," one of the students said.

For every table, Christopher had a different story, tailored to that particular set of customers. My new friend had some pretty amazing people skills. And also, as noted earlier, he was one hell of a liar.

I went to place an order and raised an eyebrow at the sight of Jamie behind the grill, flipping a burger patty. "Dear God, are you cooking?" I asked him.

"We're one line cook short because we weren't expecting a lunch rush, so I'm pitching in."

"You owe me five bucks," I said with a smile.

"What do you mean?"

"You bet me a couple years ago that you could make it to the age of twenty-five without ever actually cooking a single thing. You just lost."

Jamie grinned and handed over a five dollar bill. "I'd forgotten about that. I probably would have made it, too, if I hadn't become the owner of a bar and grill."

"Probably."

Christopher watched our exchange without comment, his intelligent blue eyes taking it all in and filing it away. Later on, as my shift was winding down and I was cleaning up my station, he asked me, "Are you still in love with Jamie?"

I stopped what I was doing and really considered the question. Then I said, "As recently as a few days ago, the answer would have been yes. Now…I do still love him, but as a friend. He'll always be important to me. But no, I'm not in love with him anymore." It was a surprising realization, and kind of freeing, actually.

"Not since you met Dante," Christopher said happily, "because you're falling in love with him."

"Oh man. There's the hopeless romantic in you again," I said as I wiped down a table.

"Not hope*less*. Hope*ful*. I want to believe that love actually exists in the world."

"Speaking of Dante," I said, slightly changing the subject, "I want to give his grandmother another call, make sure she's still okay." We went in the back and I pulled out my phone. Christopher took his out as well, scrolling through some texts as I dialed the hotel.

An accented woman's voice answered the phone in the suite, and when Mrs. Dombruso came on the line she explained, "My housekeeper Marta is here, she brought me some clothes. So is Mr. Mario. He's my hairdresser. You'd like him, Charlie. He's a gay homosexual, too."

I grinned at that and asked, "Did the doctor come by?"

"Yeah, an hour ago."

"What did he say?"

"What I already knew," she said. "I'm doing fine. Better than fine. He says I'll live to be a hundred. I said a hundred is for chumps, I'm shooting for one-ten." I reminded her to call me if she needed anything before I ended the call.

My companion finished typing a long text, then returned the phone to his pocket. "Mind if we stop by a store on the way home?" he asked me. "I'm almost out of crackers."

188

"No problem." I untied my short black apron and pulled a wad of bills from my pocket, then counted out the money and handed half of it to Christopher.

"What's that for?"

"That's your half."

"Oh no," he said, trying to hand the money back. "You did all the work. I was merely an inconvenience."

"You did plenty of work, especially by chatting up the customers. They tipped us like crazy because they were all so charmed by your outlandish tales explaining the handcuffs. Keep it, I insist."

"Well, okay. That was actually a lot of fun," he said as he slipped the money in the pocket of his jeans.

"You're a natural. If you ever want a job waiting tables, I'll put in a good word for you. Jamie would hire you in an instant."

He smiled at me. "That was really subtle. Nice work."

"What was?"

"Your little suggestion, trying to show the rent boy there's a way out of his seamy, depressing existence."

"I didn't mean it that way." Okay, I kind of had.

He took my hand and gave it a squeeze. "I don't need saving, Charlie, but I appreciate the thought."

"I just don't get why you're in that line of work," I told him honestly.

"Sutherlin costs fifty-five thousand dollars a year. I have three years left, one for my B.A., then two more for my M.F.A. Until I finish school, I'm going to keep turning tricks, because nothing else pays the kind of money I need."

"Have you looked into financial aid?"

He gave me a 'duh' expression and said, "Yeah."

"Your art would pay the bills. You're insanely talented."

"I'm also a total unknown and a student. I don't have any connections in the art world, at least not yet. Next year, I'll be eligible to intern at a couple of the local galleries. I'll be able to build a network, and that's the first step in hopefully being able to make a living from my art in the future. But I'm just not there yet."

"I worry about your safety, Christopher Robin. You're in such a dangerous line of work."

He looked at the floor and said, "Yeah, I know. It's safer now, though. Up until thirteen months ago I worked the street, and that really was dangerous. But now that I'm working for an escort service, it's not so bad. The clients are more upscale. Sure, the agency takes a big portion of my earnings. But still, it *is* safer, so it's worth the cut in pay."

"I'm sorry. I really didn't mean to lecture," I told him.

"I know. You're such a good guy, Charlie. I knew it was just a matter of time before you tried to intervene." He smiled at me fondly.

"I'm not done meddling. I want you to move in with me, be my roommate. Whatever you're paying in rent now, I'll charge you less. You need to stop living in hell."

"You have a one bedroom apartment," he pointed out.

"You can have the bedroom, I'll take the living room. I'll even throw in the Dante Collection of Fine Furnishings to sweeten the deal."

"Mr. Dombruso bought you your furniture?"

"Yeah. The first time he came to my apartment, it was almost totally empty. That didn't sit well with him."

Christopher beamed delightedly. "He's taking care of you. That's so sweet."

"Will you consider being my roommate?"

"It's a little bit crazy, you know, asking a hooker you've known for a day to move into your home."

"I like you and I trust you, Christopher. Plus, I already know you're incredibly easy to get along with. Please say yes."

"I'll think about it," he said with a grin. "Thank you for the offer."

Dmitri came into the employee dressing room and said, "Okay, spill. What exactly was Dante trying to accomplish by chaining you two together?"

"It's a kinky sex thing. Just like I told Jamie," I said.

Dmitri chuckled at that. "Liar. Is this some kind of punishment, and do you not want to tell me because I'll tell Jamie, and then he'll distrust Dante even more?"

"It's not a punishment, but you're right about the rest. Speaking of Dante, have you been in touch with him since he's been out of the country?" I asked Dmitri. "Do you know if he's doing okay?"

"I don't know, I haven't heard from him."

"He's fine," Christopher said.

I turned to look at the blond at the end of my arm. "Has Dante been in contact with you?"

"Yup. He's texted me about every two hours since his plane landed. He feels terribly guilty for doing this to you, and keeps checking to see if you're okay. I wasn't supposed to tell you," Christopher said with a big smile.

Jamie stuck his head in the locker room and asked his husband, "Has Charlie told you why he's handcuffed to a twink?" To Christopher he said, "No offense."

"That's not an insult, so much as a simple statement of fact," Christopher told him.

I sighed and decided to (sort of) come clean, going with Christopher's earlier pared down explanation that he'd given Mrs. Dombruso. "Dante chained us together. He wants me to think he's a terrible person, so I don't try to get back together with him." Obviously, I omitted the fact that Christopher was

192

supposed to be freaking me out the entire time by going into detail about Dante's sex life.

"Well, I'm convinced," Jamie said, and left the dressing room just as Cole was coming in. Dmitri grinned and followed him.

"Dude, I'm so sorry I left you short-handed at the beginning of the lunch shift," I told him.

"It's fine. Who knew we'd actually be busy?" He was looking at Christopher closely. He'd already asked about the cuffs earlier, and when I'd told him it was complicated, he just accepted that answer and moved on. Cole told him, "You remind me so much of my ex-boyfriend. But I won't hold that against you."

"You've never mentioned your ex," I said. I'd actually never even been sure Cole was gay until then.

My coworker sighed and said, "I know. He broke my heart. We moved here from Idaho with plans of building a life together. But three weeks after we got here, he dumped me. San Francisco seduced him hard and fast. I couldn't compete with every guy in every club fawning over him. These days, he's actually a big star in the porn industry, goes by the name Hunter Storm." He rolled his eyes at that, then added, "So apparently, my baby is now *everybody's* baby. How bitter does *that* sound?"

"I'm sorry, Cole."

"It's been almost two years. I keep expecting it to stop hurting, but somehow it just never does." He forced a smile and said, "On that upbeat note, I'm outta here. See you tomorrow." He grabbed his backpack and left the dressing room.

"You know," Christopher said after Cole left, "I actually get a lot of work from clients calling up and asking the agency for a Hunter Storm type."

*****

We headed back to my apartment, and after dropping off Christopher's art supplies and wrestling the dog onto his leash and out for a walk, we got in my truck and drove to the Safeway. I pushed a cart around, grabbing a couple things I'd run out of, and Christopher carried a little basket. He didn't pick up a thing, until we came to those little packs of bright orange snack crackers with peanut butter. Then he took every package off the shelf and filled his basket. "It really is the only thing I eat," he explained, when he saw my surprised expression.

"How have you not developed scurvy or something?"

"It's a mystery."

He grabbed a six-pack of bottled water as well, and I decided I wanted some ice cream, so we headed to the frozen foods aisle. But I stopped short, tugging Christopher to a stop with me. "Is something wrong?" he asked.

I didn't answer for a moment. Then I pointed at the tall, middle-aged man down at the far end of the aisle and murmured, "That's my father. He disowned me recently when I came out to him, and then my mother left him. I've never in my life seen him buying groceries. My mom used to do all the shopping and cooking."

My dad looked incredibly lost. He was pulling frozen dinners out of the freezer case and squinting at the back of them. Some went in his cart, some back into the case. The cart was full of nothing but frozen dinners.

Walter Connolly was a big guy, six-foot-two and heavy set. He was a former Marine, who still wore his graying hair in a buzz cut. He was a blue collar man, a Teamster who worked at a big newspaper printing facility. I'd never once seen even a trace of vulnerability in him. Until that moment.

"I actually feel like going over there and helping him, but I know he'd just call me a queer and tell me to get away from him," I said quietly. Christopher laced his fingers with mine and held my hand, and I sighed and left the aisle before my father saw me.

*****

Christopher and I spent the evening in my apartment. Peaches was penned back up temporarily so we could move around unmolested. I tackled the project of going through the garbage bags I'd brought from my former home, sorting my possessions into piles along the living room wall with Christopher's help.

He and I were both quiet, introspective. Seeing my dad had been jarring, and I was still trying to process it. And going through all my things, including every photo and memento from my childhood, was hard to take. I remembered how I'd broken down and cried when I first discovered all that stuff, and how Dante had held me and comforted me. God I missed him.

I took a break after a while and got a beer, and offered one to Christopher, which he declined. Instead, he got a packet of his crackers and ate them one by one as we sat on the couch, leaning against each other. Eventually he said, "Okay."

"Okay?"

"If you were serious about me moving in here as your roommate, then I accept."

"Of course I was serious."

"I think it'd be really good to live with you," Christopher said. "I'll take the living room, though. You keep the bedroom."

"We'll flip a coin for it," I said.

He put his head on my shoulder. "It's going to be really nice to move out of that residence motel."

"We can go get your stuff tomorrow, after I work the lunch shift."

He looked up at me. "You want me to move in that soon?"

"Yeah. I don't want you spending even one more night in that other place. Besides," I added with a grin, "we're never going to figure out the trick to these cuffs, so we'll be living together permanently anyway." I took another look at them and was baffled as ever.

Christopher's phone beeped and he pulled it out of his pocket to read the text, then sent a quick reply and set it on the end table.

"Not to be incredibly nosy, but was that Dante?" I asked.

"It was. Still checking up on you." He smiled happily.

"He didn't actually tell you how to open these manacles, did he?"

"Nope."

"Has he found Natori yet?"

"No. He's beginning to wonder if they're on a wild goose chase. They've been driving all over Sicily following leads, but he hasn't turned up."

"This thing he's doing scares me to death. I'm so afraid he won't come back."

"You have to think positive and believe he's going to survive this," he told me emphatically. I nodded in agreement.

"I can't begin to process the whole mafia thing, even though I understand why he feels he has to do this. As for the rest of what he does, I have no frame of reference for it, apart from the movies. And I kind of doubt The Godfather was meant to be watched as a documentary." I glanced at Christopher. "Do you know what he's involved in?"

"I only know a little about what he does, but none of the illegal stuff. I know he owns some restaurants, a couple nightclubs, a few shops. He owns a whole strip mall on the peninsula. I've gotten the impression," Christopher said, "that he's been slowly moving his family from criminal activity to legitimate sources of revenue. But I really don't know that for sure."

After a while, I sighed and said, "I'm going to keep sorting through the wreckage of my former life. I'll drag a bag over here to the couch so we can be comfortable while I bum myself out."

*****

That night, after taking turns in the shower and trying our best to respect each other's privacy while using the restroom (awkward!), Christopher and I lay facing each other in bed,

198

our joined hands between us. His eyelids were lowered and he was holding my chained hand between both of his. There was something in the way he held onto me that made me want to protect and take care of him. He put on a good show, acting like he took everything in stride, but Christopher was a lot more vulnerable than he let on. I remembered him talking about the fact that he didn't date and wondered if he was lonely.

After a while I asked, "Are you named for the character in the children's books?" It was a random question. I just wanted to get him talking.

He grinned a little and looked up at me through his thick, dark lashes. "Yeah. My mom loved those books. She read them to me over and over when I was little."

I just had to ask. "Does she know what you do for a living?"

"She killed herself when I was five." He said it quietly, but kept his voice steady.

"Oh God. I'm so sorry."

"It was a long time ago." He let go of my hand, rolled onto his back and closed his eyes.

"I can be so insensitive. I apologize for prying into your personal business."

He turned his head to look at me and offered me a little smile. "You didn't. My past is full of landmines like that one, it's sometimes hard to avoid them."

Christopher looked back up at the ceiling and said, "I might as well go ahead and clear away this landmine before you stumble across it by accident and then feel bad about it." After a long moment he said, "You've noticed my weird food thing. It started thirteen months ago. This was when I was still working the street. I always thought I had good instincts, and I thought they'd protect me. Turns out I was wrong."

He took a deep breath and said, "So, this trick bought me for an hour and took me back to his hotel room. It was right around dinnertime. He had a little cooler in the room, and he offered me a sandwich. No red flags went off. He just seemed so normal, and took one of the sandwiches for himself and started eating it. I thought, why not? I was so hungry, and it was a free meal, why pass it up?"

Christopher fell silent for a long time before beginning again, his voice quiet and level. "To this day, I have no idea what he used to drug me. I couldn't taste anything odd about that sandwich. Once I was unconscious, the man raped me and beat me almost to death, then left my body in a dumpster, presumably to die. It didn't quite work out as he'd hoped. I somehow survived. When I got out of the hospital, I stopped working the streets and went to work for the escort service."

"Did the police catch him?" My voice was a ragged whisper.

"No. I doubt they looked very hard. I mean, what's one raped and beaten prostitute?"

"Oh God," I whispered.

He went on, "That's when I stopped eating. Food started to freak me out. I'd try to eat something and I'd just start gagging, I couldn't make myself swallow anything. Eventually, I stumbled upon those crackers by chance, and found that for some reason, I could tolerate them. They don't trigger my gag reflex, so I can actually swallow them. I don't know why."

Christopher sighed and sat up, looking down at me. "That's the long, pathetic story of my food phobia. In short, I'm a fucking mess. But I'm managing to survive and not starve myself to death. For right now…well, that's all I'm really shooting for."

I sat up and tried to hug him, totally overcome with emotion, but he stopped me with a raised palm. "Don't be nice to me right now, Charlie. If you do, I'm just going to start crying, and that's something I generally avoid at all costs."

We both laid back down, staring up at the ceiling in the semi-darkness. After a long time like that, Christopher rolled over so he was facing me, slid close and rested his head on my chest. Wordlessly, I put my free arm around him and held him until he fell asleep.

Chapter Fourteen

Lunchtime at Nolan's was apparently starting to catch on. The next day at work, I'd been going nonstop for a couple hours and was right in the middle of the dining room, juggling an armload of dirty plates, when my phone rang. "Want me to get that for you?" Christopher asked.

"Yeah, it might be important. Mrs. Dombruso might need something."

Christopher fished the phone out of my pocket and showed me Dante's name on the screen before hitting the speaker icon and holding it up to me. "Hi, Dante!" I said cheerfully.

Dante's weak, shaking voice sent a jolt of panic through me. "Charlie," he whispered. "My angel. I'm so sorry."

"Dante, what's wrong? Why are you apologizing?"

"I'm so sorry I broke up with you, Charlie. I wanted to be with you more than anything. But I thought it was for your own good." I heard him shift slightly and gasp in pain.

Fear slammed into me so hard that I couldn't draw a breath. "Dante, what's happened?"

He spoke slowly, in short, choppy sentences. "I got him. I got the man that killed my family. But he got me, too. He shot me. I'm not gonna survive this."

"Where are you? Are there people around? Can you get help?" I was vaguely aware of someone taking the dishes from me, and I grabbed the phone from Christopher.

"No one's here. I'm all alone." His breathing was becoming labored, and I clutched the phone with both hands. I barely noticed as Christopher reached up and did something to the manacle, releasing it from my wrist. "I have to tell you something. I have to tell you I love you, Charlie. I need you to know that. I love you so much."

"I love you too Dante, and I can't lose you! You have to get help!" My body shook as Christopher hugged me tightly.

"You love me?" His voice was barely a whisper.

"Yes. God I love you."

"Oh angel."

"Dante, you have to hang up and dial nine-one-one. Or whatever nine-one-one is in Sicily. You have to do that now!"

He sounded so young as he said, "I don't want to die alone. Please Charlie, stay on the phone with me. I want to hear your voice. I need every moment I have left to be with you."

"Dante, you have to try to get help! You have to call an ambulance." I looked up, realizing that not only was this conversation on speaker, but every single person in the bar was staring at me, wide-eyed and hanging on every word. I yelled to the crowd, "How do you call an ambulance in Sicily? What number do you dial?"

Several people including Jamie and Dmitri, who were right beside me, whipped out phones and started frantically searching the internet. In just a few seconds a stranger waved his phone and shouted, "One-one-eight! That's what he has to dial for an ambulance!"

"Dante, you have to dial one-one-eight. Do you hear me? You have to try to get help."

"Don't want to hang up."

I said, "You have to. You have to hang up and then you have to dial one-one-eight."

"No. Stay with me, Charlie. Please." His voice was a faint whisper.

"I need you to get help, Dante." I pressed my eyes shut and said, "I'm going to hang up. I want you to dial one-one-eight the moment we get off the phone. Then I'm going to call you back in one minute."

"No. Don't go."

"Tell me what you're going to dial when I hang up." I tried to make my voice firm, even as I shattered with despair.

"One…one…eight?"

"Yes. I love you, Dante. I'll call you back in one minute." I ended the call.

I turned to Christopher and whispered, "Oh God, what did I just do? What if he dies? He wanted me to stay with him. What if he dies in the next minute? I'll never forgive myself for hanging up on him!"

Christopher pulled me against him, clutching me fiercely. His voice was shaking as he said, "You did the right thing, Charlie. That was his only chance. You have to believe he's calling for help right now. It was the only thing that could save him."

I shook and clung to my friend for just a minute, and then I let go, took a deep breath and called Dante back. It was on speaker again, and everyone in the bar held their breath as the phone rang once…twice…three times. On the fourth ring, voice mail picked up. I disconnected and tried again as fear trickled ice cold through my body. Again I got voice mail. I tried again. And again. And again. It went on like that for several minutes, and each time I got the same result.

I completely lost it then, crying so hysterically that I could barely breathe. "Let's get him home," someone said. Strong arms were around me, supporting me. I'm not sure what exactly happened after that.

*****

Eventually I realized I was back home, seated on my couch, clinging to Christopher like he was the only thing anchoring me to the earth. I gradually became aware of other people around me as the tears tapered off and were replaced with a cold, aching emptiness. Jamie sat beside me, his hand on my shoulder. Dmitri paced nearby, placing call after call, trying to get information on Dante. Jess sat on the loveseat with a laptop computer, and every time Dmitri hung up, Jess would recite another number, which Dmitri dialed. He'd then say something into the phone in choppy Italian. The only words I could make out were Dante Dombruso.

A gentle hand on my knee made me focus my attention on the person in front of me. Callie sat on the edge of the coffee table, holding a glass of water. "Are you really here?" I asked her, reaching out a fingertip to touch her auburn hair.

"Yes Charlie, I'm here. Jess and I came right over when Jamie texted her. Here sweetie, try to drink a little water."

I tried to take the glass, but my hand was shaking too hard. Christopher took it for me and held it to my lips, and I managed a couple choking sips.

Jamie was brushing tears off my face with the back of his hand. He said, "Dmitri and Jess are calling every hospital in Sicily. And Dmitri called Dante's men, they're all trying to find him."

I nodded, wrapping my arms tightly around Christopher. "Don't let go of me," I whispered to him.

"Not a chance, Charlie." He kissed my forehead.

"He can't be dead," I mumbled as he rubbed my back. "He just can't be. We just found each other. I can't lose him already."

"We don't know what happened," Christopher said. "So don't give up, Charlie. I'll help you hold on to hope."

Chapter Fifteen

My life felt like a nightmare that I couldn't wake up from. It had been seventeen hours since Dante's phone call. My friends stayed with me in shifts, except for Jamie and Christopher, who stayed with me constantly. I didn't sleep and couldn't eat. The only thing I did was lay in bed staring at my phone, which was plugged in on my nightstand.

Christopher went to the kitchen and Jamie sat down beside me on the mattress, the two of them working out a wordless choreography to make sure I was never left alone. Jamie brushed my hair back from my forehead and said softly, "You need to try to rest, Charlie. You won't miss anything. The phone's right there, and if it rings, it'll wake you. *I'll* wake you. I'll sit right here while you sleep."

I shook my head, staring intently at the phone, as if concentrating hard enough would somehow make it ring. "Go home to your husband, Jamie," I murmured.

"I'm not going anywhere until I know you're okay, Charlie."

"But I'm never going to be okay. Not if he's gone. I don't know how I'll survive it."

"I'll help you. You'll get through it," he said.

Christopher came back then, climbing up onto the bed and snuggling against me. He rested a little bowl on his leg and hand-fed me something that I didn't taste as he said, "We still don't know what happened. We're not going to give up hope." He shot Jamie a look as he fed me another bit of food.

*****

Hours dragged, one after the other in a painfully slow procession. I started to doze just a little, despite myself, until the ringing of my phone jarred me awake. I grabbed it so quickly that I almost knocked over the lamp on my nightstand. Jamie's hand shot out to catch it as I fumbled with the on button and blurted, "Hello?"

"Charlie. My angel."

"Dante?" I yanked the power cord out of the phone and sat bolt upright, praying this wasn't a dream.

"God, it's good to hear your voice." His own voice was faint, groggy, scratchy. It was the most wonderful thing I'd ever heard in my entire life.

"Darling, where are you?"

"Rome. In a hospital. Just woke up from surgery. Had to call you right away."

"Dante, what happened?"

"Was shot." He sounded even groggier, as if talking was wearing him out. "Called an ambulance, like you said. Guess they found me. How long was I out?"

"Almost—" I looked at the clock, "—twenty-three hours. The longest of my life."

"Nurse is trying to take the phone away. I'll call you soon, okay?" I heard a woman's voice speaking to him in agitated Italian, and then the line went dead.

"He's alive. Thank God he's alive," I told my friends, overcome with relief and gratitude.

"Where is he?" Jamie asked. He was sitting at my bedside, looking tired and rumpled in clothes from a day ago.

"A hospital in Rome. He just came out of surgery."

Christopher smiled at me. "If he's strong enough to call, he's obviously doing okay. I'm so happy for you, Charlie."

Jamie sent a quick text, and then he stood up and said, "I just told Dmitri that Dante checked in from a Roman hospital. He'll tell Dante's men to call off the hunt. I'm going to go home and get some sleep, unless you need anything, Charlie."

I shook my head. "Thanks for staying with me, Jamie, you're a good friend. Please thank Dmitri, Callie, and Jess for me, too."

He reached out and squeezed my shoulder. "I will."

After he left, Christopher took my phone from my hands and plugged it back in on the nightstand, then turned the light off and pulled the covers over both of us. "Thank you for being so strong for me, Christopher Robin," I murmured, kissing the top of his head. "I don't know how I would have gotten through that without you."

"I didn't really do anything," he whispered, already falling asleep. "But you're welcome."

*****

The next time he called, it was almost eighteen hours later. I snatched my ringing phone off the nightstand and answered it with, "Dante?"

"Hi angel. Sorry it took me so long to call back. They gave me something that knocked me out."

I grinned and said, "You sound a lot better."

"Was I even speaking in complete sentences when I called before? The anesthesia hadn't really worn off yet." Dante's voice was still a bit thin and his breathing was slightly labored.

"You were, actually. How do you feel?"

"Like I've been shot four times."

"Oh God."

"I'll tell you all about it when I see you."

"When will that be?" I asked, expecting him to say it would be days or weeks before he was well enough to travel.

"In about fourteen hours." He drew in his breath as if something was hurting him, then let it out slowly.

"*What*? They didn't really let you out of the hospital already, did they?"

"I wouldn't exactly describe it as *let me*, but I am out of the hospital and on my way to the airport."

"Dante, you've been shot. You just had surgery!" I exclaimed. "What are you doing?"

"I'm coming home to you, angel, and once I get there, I'm never leaving your side again. I was so fucking stupid to break up with you. I need to be with you."

"But it's too soon! You're going to hurt yourself."

"I'll be fine."

"So, it must be a Dombruso thing," I said, knitting my brows. "I thought it was just your grandmother. But apparently the whole family has a pathological need to flee hospitals."

He chuckled a little, then said, "Ow."

"How are you getting to the airport? Don't tell me you hopped in a cab!"

"No, I'm on a stretcher in an ambulance, hooked to an IV. I hired a doctor and two nurses to come with me on the plane I chartered, to make sure I survive the flight."

"Dante, this sounds incredibly risky. You need to go back to the hospital!"

"I'll check into a hospital when I get to San Francisco. The medical team will keep me stable until then."

"Dante, why are you doing this? I'm so afraid you're going to hurt yourself. Why are you in such a hurry to come back here?"

"I told you, Charlie. I need to be with you."

"That's not enough of a reason to take chances with your health like this!"

"I'm doing this as safely as I can, angel, and I *am* coming home to you. I won't spend one more night apart from you."

I sighed and said, "You're epically stubborn. Do you know this about yourself?"

I could hear the smile in his voice when he said, "I do know that. Do you know I'm completely in love with you?"

Now it was my turn to smile. "Yeah? You're sticking with that, even now that you don't think you're dying?"

He chuckled a little, but it quickly turned into a grunt of pain. He said, "I love you, Charlie. Thinking I was dying only accelerated telling you what I've been feeling for a while."

"I love you too, Dante. When I thought I'd lost you, my whole world ended."

"I'm so sorry to worry you like that. And I'm so sorry for breaking up with you, and for chaining you to Austin. God, I was an asshole. I'm so sorry for all of it." After a moment he added quietly, "I'm sorry for putting my need for revenge ahead of you, knowing it could get me killed."

"I understand why you had to do that," I said. "Is it over now? Is Natori dead?"

"Yes, he's dead. But so are a lot of other people. He killed all three of the men I brought with me. They were good men, and they died for my vendetta," he said, his voice full of regret. "There's been so much blood spilled. So much. But no more. I accomplished what I needed to do, and now I'm retiring, I'm handing the family business over to my cousins. I'm through."

He gasped in pain, and I asked frantically, "Are you okay, Dante?"

"Yeah. The ambulance just hit a rut in the road."

"Where are you hurt?"

"I was shot in the left arm and the right wrist, and both those bullets broke bones. I have casts on each arm. Another bullet passed through my chest cavity, but missed all my organs. A fourth lodged in my thigh and severed a major artery, but the surgeons patched it up."

"Oh my God! How are you even holding the phone?"

"I'm not," he said. "I'm wearing a headset."

"I can't believe you're travelling in that condition. It's insanely risky."

"The only risk is letting you see me like this. I really can't imagine why you'd still want me once you see me this pathetic and broken. But I'm swallowing my pride and rushing home to you anyway Charlie, because I miss you so much." His voice was getting really raspy, and was made even worse by clearing his throat. "We're pulling up to the airport now."

"Have you made plans for your arrival at SFO?"

"Yeah. A private ambulance will be taking me to Rosewood. Maybe I'll get Nana's old room," he said lightly.

"Call me as soon as you're on the ground."

"I will, angel."

When we finally said our goodbyes, I fell back onto the bed. He was coming home. He was probably totally endangering his health by doing that, but my Dante was coming home to me.

Chapter Sixteen

Christopher Robin and I had been playing canasta with Mrs. Dombruso all evening in the lobby at Rosewood. She'd roped in a little old man to be our fourth, and we were no match for the senior card sharks. Finally, Mr. Previn was ordered back to bed by one of the nurses, and we had to call it quits.

I sat beside Mrs. Dombruso, not really watching the local news and glancing at the time every few seconds. "He ought to be landing soon," she said, noting my restlessness and patting my hand. Dante's flight had faced weather delays at foggy SFO, so I didn't know if he was on the ground yet.

"I can't believe he's doing this. What if he had a medical emergency while on the plane? He's taking such a risk. He should have stayed in Rome until he was a little more stable," I ranted, not for the first time.

"He misses his sweetie pie," she said. He'd called her that morning as well and had told her he was rushing home to me.

"I miss him too, but I'm worried sick. What if his condition took a turn for the worse while he was in the air? But he's so stubborn, he wouldn't be talked out of this terrible idea."

"You'd better get used to stubborn, Charlie."

Christopher returned with some snacks from the vending machine. "Did you bring me something?" she asked him.

"Yes ma'am," Christopher said, handing her a couple candy bars. She stashed one in the pocket of her purple velour track suit (which came with a matching bedazzled purple velour baseball cap) and unwrapped the other. We'd discovered over the course of the evening that Mrs. Dombruso had a raging sweet tooth and a penchant for junk food.

My phone rang and I lunged for it, knocking it off the armrest of my chair. I snatched it up with a breathless, "Dante?"

"Hi, angel."

I sighed with relief and slumped in my chair. "Hi sweetheart. How do you feel?"

"Not bad. The doctor gave me something that knocked me out for most of the flight."

I grinned and said, "You sound a little loopy."

"Yeah, sedatives and narcotic painkillers will do that to ya."

"Are you still at the airport?"

"Nope. I would have called sooner, but I just woke up a minute ago."

"So where are you?"

"I'm right here, Charlie." That came not from the phone, but from the double doors that had just slid open.

I dropped the phone and raced to his side. Dante was pale and exhausted-looking. He was on a stretcher pushed by a nurse, with tubes, machines and bandages everywhere. But he was also smiling. I simultaneously burst out laughing and crying, all my worry and fear colliding with my relief. Dante reached under his blanket and pulled out a clean, white, monogrammed handkerchief, holding it up to me between the index and middle fingers of his broken right hand. I laughed and cried even harder as I took the handkerchief from him and wiped my eyes.

I leaned over and kissed him, lightly, carefully. He moaned against my lips and returned the kiss urgently, passionately, as I held his face between my hands. When we finally broke apart, I looked into his beautiful dark eyes and whispered, "I love you, Dante."

He smiled up at me, his eyes sparkling even through the narcotic haze, and said, "I love you too, angel."

"What are all of you looking at?" Mrs. Dombruso demanded from somewhere close behind me. "So my grandson is a gay homosexual. You got a problem with that? If so, you can all go fuck yourselves."

I glanced up and realized we had quite an audience. Several doctors and nurses crowded the lobby, all in various stages of embarrassment. In the past, that would have mortified me, but right then I really didn't give a shit. I only cared that my Dante was with me.

"Hi Nana," Dante said with a drugged up grin. "Hi Austin." I looked over my shoulder and saw Mrs. Dombruso leaning on Christopher, her arm linked with his. He was grinning at me happily.

"The boy's name is Christopher Robin," Mrs. Dombruso corrected.

"It is? I didn't realize," said Dante, knitting his brows as his foggy brain tried to make sense of that.

It took over half an hour for the medical team to get Dante set up in his room and perform a thorough check of all his vital signs. I sat in a chair in the corner and watched as the Italian doctor explained in choppy English and elaborate hand gestures the extent of Dante's injuries to the three American doctors. Mrs. Dombruso bustled in and kissed her grandson on the forehead before swearing at him for a good ten minutes for flying home in his condition.

When she finally ran out of steam, Christopher and I escorted her to the front of the hospital and helped her hail a cab. She was obviously exhausted by the stress of the past few days, and had dark circles under her watery brown eyes. "He was a damn fool to fly so soon," she griped. "But thank God he's home."

Once she was deposited in a cab, Christopher turned to me and said, "Well, I guess you don't need me anymore." He looked a little lost.

I pulled him into a hug and said, "Like hell I don't."

He held on to me and said quietly, "But your boyfriend's back now, and we're not chained together anymore."

"About that. When did you figure out how to open the manacles?"

"Um…within ninety seconds of examining them, that first night we spent together."

"Why didn't you remove them sooner?"

"I'm so sorry, Charlie. I just…I wanted to stay with you. I know that sounds stupid and pathetic, but I liked being with you. I wanted to have our forty-eight hours together, before we went our separate ways."

I pulled back to look at him and he avoided my gaze, so I gently took his chin and tilted his face up to mine, my arm still around his shoulders. "We're not going our separate ways."

His big blue eyes searched my face. "We're not?"

"Nope. You're my new roommate, remember? You agreed to move in with me."

"Why would you still want that, especially after I tricked you, made you stay chained to me?"

"Why? Because you're my best friend," I told him.

"I am?"

"That can't be news to you, Christopher Robin. After everything we've been through together? After the million ways you've been there for me? Of course you are."

He smiled at that and put his arms around me again, resting his head on my chest. "You're mine too, Charlie."

I kissed the top of his head and held him for a while before finally letting go of him and handing him my house key. "I'm going to try to spend the night here if the staff lets me. You should go home to our apartment and get some rest."

"Ok, roomie. See you when you get home." He smiled at me warmly before turning and heading down the street.

The doctors were just leaving, still engrossed in conversation, as I returned to Dante's room. "Hi angel," he said with a big grin. I started to sit on the chair beside the bed, and he said, "What are you doing? Come here." He was laying on his right side, and gestured with his chin to the bed beside him.

"That seems like a really bad idea," I said. "I don't want to jostle you." I reached out and brushed his silky black hair back from his forehead.

"Please?"

I sighed and kicked my shoes off, then gingerly got up on the mattress beside him. "I can't resist when you ask so nicely." I carefully laid on my side, sharing his pillow, his face inches from mine.

"Hi," he said softly, with a sweet smile.

"Hi Dante." I was smiling, too.

His dark eyes searched my face. "My beautiful angel," he murmured. "Do you have any idea how much I missed you?"

"I have some idea, given the fact that you just jeopardized your health to come home to me."

He leaned forward so his forehead was resting against mine and let his eyes slide shut. "Totally worth the risk."

I started to reach out to him, but stopped myself. "I don't know where I can touch you."

"Go ahead and take a look. I'd say it looks worse than it is, but I guess I'd be lying."

I sat up and pulled the covers back. His left arm was in a cast to mid-bicep, a sling holding it against his stomach, tubes from an IV running into his upper arm. His right hand was in a cast to mid-forearm. His left thigh was bandaged knee to hip, and surgical tape was wound around his chest, holding a big square of gauze in place. I drew in my breath and met his gaze. "How close did the bullet come to your heart, Dante?"

He hesitated and then admitted, "An inch."

"Holy shit."

"Come here, Charlie," he said gently. I lay down again, pulling the blanket over both of us and sliding my fingers into his hair, my forehead against his again.

"I almost lost you."

"But you didn't. I'm here."

"Thank God," I whispered.

I ended up spending all night in Dante's hospital bed, despite the protests of the medical staff. They only backed off when Dante threatened to buy the hospital and fire all of them. He tried to tell me he'd never be able to sleep in the hospital, but sheer exhaustion and the powerful painkillers knocked him out within a few minutes. I watched over him for a long time, before I too drifted off.

*****

In the morning, Dante's forehead was creased with concern. "Are you okay?" I asked him, sitting up and quickly looking him over.

"I didn't think this through," he said quietly.

"Didn't think what through?"

"Coming home to you in this condition."

"Why? Are you in pain? Should I get the doctor?"

He shook his head. "No angel, I'm alright. I'm getting a steady drip of painkillers from my IV, so I don't feel much of anything." It occurred to me that even if he was in excruciating pain, Dante really wasn't the type of man to admit it. I'd have to keep a close eye on him, make sure he really was doing okay and not just putting up a brave front.

"Then what's wrong?" I asked, brushing his hair out of his eyes.

"I'm ridiculously helpless with these casts on each arm. I didn't think about what that would mean during my recovery."

"It's going to be okay, Dante. I'll help you."

"That's just it. I want you to know you don't have to take care of me. You're not under any obligation—"

"Of course I'm going to take care of you," I said.

"Maybe that's not the best idea…."

"Sure it is."

He hesitated for a long moment, and then he admitted quietly, "I'm so fucking scared of losing you, Charlie. I can't imagine why you'd want me when I'm so pathetic and broken. And I'm worried about being a burden to you, that having to deal with me in this condition day after day is going to drive you away."

"I'm not going anywhere, Dante. I love you. It's like I tried to tell you before, I'm all in with this relationship. That means in sickness and in health, in good times and bad. I'm going to help you heal, and we're going to be together, because it's what we both want."

"I do want that. God I want that," he murmured, and leaned in and kissed me gently.

Chapter Seventeen

For the last five weeks, Dante and I and Christopher Robin and the zombie lap dog from hell had lived as one big, odd family in my little apartment. It had been…interesting.

When Dante decided to step down from his role as the head of his 'family business', he also decided to move out of the big villa on Nob Hill and had most of his personal belongings put in storage. It was the headquarters for mob operations, and always crowded with family members and business associates. It made sense to turn it over along with the job. He held on to enough of his legitimate investment properties that money was never going to be an issue for him.

Dante and Christopher were adapting to their new role as roommates. It was a little awkward at first, but they were always unfailingly polite to one another. Christopher was learning to address Dante by his first name, while Dante only occasionally called him Austin.

They'd taken on the project of trying to civilize Peaches, a task I gave up on in the first five minutes of that little experiment. Dante mostly acted as a consultant since he couldn't do much physically, looking up dog training videos on his phone and coming up with ideas and theories. Dante and Christopher were bonding well against their common enemy.

Their biggest success to date had been managing to brush Peaches' teeth, which had involved wrapping the dog up in a blanket like a big burrito, then using a toothbrush duct taped to the end of a broom handle to swipe at his teeth while he snarled and snapped. It was a total triumph in that everyone still had all their fingers at the end of it, and the dog's breath actually improved slightly. Very slightly. Christopher had actually tried to take the dog to the vet for a professional cleaning, but Peaches had gone so psychotic when they went to tranquilize him that they'd been asked to leave. I tried to tell him that would happen.

Dante had been in pretty bad shape for the first couple weeks following surgery, but every day he grew stronger. He still couldn't do a lot even five weeks later, especially with the casts on his arms, but he seemed to be in much less pain. He never complained, but I'd learned to read the quiet signs, the tightening around his eyes when he was suffering, the set of his jaw.

I'd taken a leave of absence from work and was Dante's constant companion, his nurse, his cook, his valet, whatever he needed. Jamie and Dmitri and Jess and Callie had worked out some sort of schedule, and one or more of them appeared every couple days with baked goods, DVDs, flowers, magazines, little ways to brighten our days and keep our spirits up. I was so grateful for my friends.

My newest friend Christopher Robin and I bonded over, of all things, football. It turned out that he was a huge Atlanta Falcons fan. He and I developed a good-natured rivalry and watched every NFL game obsessively on the big new TV Dante bought for the apartment (while Dante tried and failed to pretend he was interested in the sport).

When Christopher gushed about the Falcons, he'd start to slip into a slight southern drawl. It only came out when he was really excited or upset or tired and forgot to rein it in. He finally admitted that he'd grown up in Georgia, but had spent all of his adult life trying to shake the accent. He didn't seem to want to talk about his time in the south.

There were two Christophers (neither of which ate much). One was the laid-back art student who dressed in baggy t-shirts and jeans. That Cristopher spent his time either sketching in a patch of sunlight on the living room floor, or hanging out with us and chatting animatedly about pretty much anything. The other was the prostitute who grew serious when it was time to go out on an assignment, donning his tight, revealing 'work clothes' with studied indifference, double-checking his pockets for condoms and then leaving with a smile that looked real, but that never reached his big blue eyes.

He didn't talk about his job, and I didn't ask. I tried to be okay with what he did for a living, even though I feared for his safety and worried about what it was doing to his sense of

226

self-worth. On days when he came home and went straight into the bathroom without a word and soaked in a tub of hot water for over an hour, my heart broke for him.

I talked to Dante about it. He wanted to pay Christopher's tuition so he could quit working, but when we brought up the subject with Christopher, he got really angry and told us he refused to accept charity. Later on, he apologized. But he still refused to take the money.

Dante wasn't done trying to intervene, though. One random Thursday night he announced that he was going have a friend over for dinner, and asked Christopher to join us. The visit was preceded by a caterer. He prepared a lavish meal for us while Peaches went full Cujo, hackles raised, growling menacingly and trying to bust out of his pen the entire time the man was preparing the meal. By the time the caterer left, all the Peaches trauma had resulted in a pronounced facial tic. Dante paid him double.

When Christopher went to open the door for our guest, he gasped and stammered, his southern accent as thick as I'd ever heard it, "Oh ma gawd, it's Ian Tremont! If this is a dream, nobody pinch me!"

I learned that Ian Tremont owned the most famous art gallery in all of San Francisco, and was a poker buddy of Dante's. Christopher's paintings dotted our apartment, and Tremont was instantly captivated by them. Within minutes, he gave Christopher his business card and asked him to be a part of his gallery's annual new artists show in January. Over dinner, the two of them went on and on about art. Christopher hung on Ian's every word, and vice versa.

I began to get the impression that Tremont was as interested in the artist as his art, and I took a long look at the gallery owner. He was a handsome man of about thirty, with grey eyes that crinkled at the corners when he smiled, and tidy light brown hair and impeccable clothes. Christopher was completely focused on him, almost mesmerized. There seemed to be a little something between them, a spark that went beyond mutual admiration, which for some reason surprised me.

After dinner Dante feigned exhaustion, and he and I retired to our bedroom while Ian and Christopher moved to the couch and kept talking. I kissed my boyfriend on the cheek and said, "That was really nice of you."

"Christopher deserves an opportunity like this, and it was easy enough to introduce them." Dante exhaled slowly and settled against the pillows.

"Are you in pain? Do you want your meds?" I asked as I sat beside him and took his hand.

"No thanks, I'm fine."

I curled up beside him, and he brushed my hair back from my forehead. It was getting kind of shaggy since I hadn't done much for myself over the last five weeks, including trips to the barber. Dante studied me closely, something he did often, a little smile on his gorgeous lips as he said, "When I'm fully recovered, I want to take you someplace wonderful as a thank you for all you've been doing for me. Maybe Fiji, someplace warm and tropical."

"Sounds nice," I murmured, and kissed his fingertips as he lightly traced my lips. He more or less had the use of his right hand, the cast beginning at the base of his fingers. He'd found he could feed himself and take care of most basic needs with that hand, while the other was completely useless in a big cast to his fingertips.

He leaned in and kissed me, slowly and deeply. Over the last month, Dante and I had spent countless hours talking, and in later weeks, when he felt a bit better, countless more hours making out like teenagers. Our time together had been sweet and tender and romantic, and it had been wonderful to really get to know him.

Of course, since he'd been so badly hurt, we'd steered clear of anything sexual whatsoever. My only outlet was the time I spent in the shower every morning, releasing twenty-four hours' worth of sexual tension across the tile wall. So when Dante's hand slid to my ass I was a little startled, and I looked up at him curiously. "Will you do something for me, Charlie?" he asked.

"Of course. Anything."

He grinned at me and said, "Take your clothes off."

"We can't mess around, Dante. You're not well enough."

229

"You're right that we can't fuck, and we still have to have a very long discussion about how we're going to have sex once I'm healed. The basic issue still remains. I don't want to hurt you, and I can't get off any other way. But I'm not opening that can of worms right now. I'm just asking you to get naked."

"If that's what you want," I said with a smile. I stripped myself quickly and stretched out on my back, looking up at him. His fingers traced my skin, circling my nipples before meandering down to my navel, then down my happy trail. My cock was already half-hard, and when he ran a fingertip over my slit, I gasped. He slid his fingers down my shaft and caressed my balls, and I let out a low moan.

Dante smiled and said, "Your best friend and a major player in the art world are right on the other side of that door. You need to be quiet, angel."

"Then maybe you should stop playing with me," I whispered with a grin.

He pretended to consider that, then said, "No, I think I'll keep doing this. In fact, please bring me the briefcase that's in the bottom of the closet, Charlie."

I rolled off the bed and did as he asked. I set the case on the mattress and popped it open, and a nervous laugh burst from me. "And here I'd assumed this was full of paperwork." What it contained instead was a whole bunch of sex toys. There were dildos and butt plugs and some things I actually couldn't name. My cock throbbed in anticipation, and I asked, "Are you really feeling up to this, Dante?"

"Yup."

"You sure?"

"I want to give you pleasure, Charlie. You need more than a daily release in the shower."

"Oh man. Can you hear me when I play with myself?" I felt the color rising in my cheeks.

"It's the highlight of my morning," he said with a smile.

I grinned embarrassedly and said, "So, what do you propose we do with this stuff?"

"Normally, I'd just have you lay back and have all manner of wonderful, dirty things done to you. But since I can only use one hand, and just barely, this is going to have to be much more collaborative."

"I have to ask," I said, peering into the case. "In the past, did you take this portable sex kit with you when you travelled, and did you ever go through airport security with it? Because that had to be entertaining."

"Nope. It was all selected specifically for you."

"Wait. You had workers pack up your playroom and put it in storage when you moved out of your house. Who did you send in to put together a sex kit for me? And oh my God, if you say it was your pal Dmitri, I'm going to kill myself!"

"God no. Like I'd want Dmitri, and by extension, your ex, involved in any of our private business."

"Well thank God. But then who packed the case?"

"It wasn't packed from my playroom. This was all newly purchased at a sex shop."

"Oh. By who?"

"Christopher."

I face-planted onto the mattress and moaned.

"Your best friend is a prostitute, angel. He was also my long-time sex partner. He's extremely well-versed in what I like sexually, and in fact, in all things sex-related, and was very businesslike in putting this kit together. Also, as your friend, he was very careful to look out for your best interests. He made sure not to select anything too extreme, too large, or too hard for you to handle."

"Nothing totally humiliating about any of that," I groaned, still burying my face in the mattress.

"It just depends on how you look at it."

I sat up and pulled a medium-sized blue butt plug out of the case. "My best friend picked this out, knowing it was going to be used on me. How is that not humiliating?"

"Actually," Dante said, his voice surprisingly soft, "it's really touching that he included that model. It's a personal favorite of his. I used to have one just like it in the playroom and I'd use it on him as a reward, after particularly brutal sessions. It always soothed him and made him feel really good."

"Wow. That's more than I ever wanted to know about the two of you, and it's still super weird that Christopher did this shopping for you. For us."

"I'm really sorry. We can throw all of this out if you want and we can shop for different stuff," he told me.

"I don't think about it much," I said, pulling a pillow onto my lap and hugging it, "the fact that you and my best friend had sex like, a hundred times. I can't give it much thought, because if I do, it just sort of freaks me out."

"For him, it was business. For me…well, this'll sound awful, but he was just a way of getting off. I never loved him. We never had a relationship. We just fucked. And it all happened before I met you, Charlie."

"I know. He told me you cancelled on him the night you met me." I grinned and added, "Little did you know you wouldn't be getting any for *weeks* after that."

He grinned too. "From the first night I met you, I never wanted anyone else."

I turned the blue toy over in my hand and was quiet for a while, mulling over my boyfriend's and my best friend's history. It was only weird if I let it be. The two of them were dealing with it, after all, managing to live cordially as roommates without letting the past cloud the present. I too could choose to just accept it and move on, like they had. Eventually I said, "I don't get why this would be a favorite. It looks like any other plug."

"I could show you what makes it special, if you like."

I handed him the toy and made a decision. I wasn't going to let the past throw me off, and I wasn't going to let Christopher's involvement in packing this case freak me out. I was just going to enjoy my first sexual encounter with Dante in weeks, and not ruin it with misplaced jealousy and insecurity. I tossed the pillow I was holding aside and laid back and spread my legs. "Okay. Show me."

"Oh. In you?" Dante looked surprised.

"Yeah. I'm done being weird about it. Show me what it does. In fact, show me what everything in that case does. Use it all on me."

He smiled and said, "It'll take me days to use all of that on you, but we can certainly start with this."

He took a sealed package of lube from the case and said, "As I said earlier, this has to be a collaborative effort. Please get a couple towels from the bathroom for me, Charlie." I did as he asked and was back a moment later, my cock already starting to sit up and take notice. "Spread one towel out on the mattress and tear open this package. Then put a lot of lube on the index and middle finger of your left hand. Coat them thoroughly on all sides."

"Oh God," I gasped as I realized what was happening. My cock throbbed in response.

"Lay on your back, angel, and spread your legs wide. Then slowly and carefully work one finger into your little hole for me."

There was something so fucking hot about being directed like that, about the quiet, confident way Dante was assuming control. I complied immediately with a murmured, "Yes sir." I rocked back so my butt was in the air, knees on my chest, and reached around to my ass. He liked that. His lips parted slightly and his hand went to his cock, stroking it lightly through his clothes as I rubbed my little opening with a slick finger and then pushed it inside me.

I had never fingered myself before, and was surprised at just how tight I was. I couldn't imagine how Dante's big, thick cock would ever fit inside me. But now wasn't the time for random musings, and I pushed deeper into myself. I did it too fast, and gasped at a sudden jolt of discomfort. Dante soothed me and coached me to go more slowly.

Eventually I took all of my finger inside me, the rest of my hand cupping my ass. I moaned quietly and rocked on my hand, fucking myself as Dante reached over and caressed my cock and balls. Embarrassingly, I made a sound that was not unlike a purr.

He rubbed his thumb over the precum on the tip of my cock, then took the hand I was using to finger myself. He couldn't make a fist with the cast on, but he could grasp with his thumb and fingers, and he held my hand firmly as he instructed, "Work the second finger in, angel."

"Yes sir." I was way too aroused to be gentle with myself, and shoved the second finger inside me along with the first, biting my lip to stop myself from crying out. Then I got why Dante was holding onto me. He began to use my hand like a dildo, fucking my ass with my own fingers. "Oh God yes," I whispered, rocking up off the mattress, grabbing a fistful of sheets with my free hand.

A knock on the bedroom door froze us both like an erotic statue. The door opened an inch and Christopher called, "Don't worry, I'm not coming in. Ian's outside bringing his car around. He and I are going for coffee, or you know, bottled water in my case. So you can give up on the terrible job you're doing of not making any noise. Did y'all not see the gags I packed in that case? Now what do you suppose those are for, people?" Christopher chuckled and added, "I'll be gone at least a couple hours. Have fun!" He closed the door behind him.

Dante and I both burst out laughing, and then he slowly started working my ass again. Within a minute we were right back where we had been, but this time with plenty of moaning. "Want to cum this way, angel?" Dante asked me.

I shook my head. "I want that plug. I want everything in that briefcase. Please!"

Dante grinned and slid my hand out of me, and gave me the second towel. As I wiped my hand he squirted some lube on the plug and rubbed it around with his fingers, then picked it up and pushed it into me. I was already so loosened up that it popped right in, even the wide, flared section. "Mmmmm," I purred, wiggling my ass on it. "Feels good. So nice and full."

"It does more than just fill you up," he said. "Much more." I couldn't begin to guess what that meant, until he picked up a little remote control and held it where I could see it. "It has a surprisingly powerful motor. There are ten settings. One through three are the nice, soothing settings I mentioned earlier. Four through six will make you cum violently."

"What about seven plus?"

"No idea. You'll never make it past six without cumming."

"Sounds like a challenge. What else is in that case?" I asked, propping myself up on my elbows and grinning broadly.

"These," he said with a smile, tossing the manacles that had joined Christopher and me onto the bed.

"You know, I never did figure out how to open them."

"Good," he said cheerfully. "Then I can keep using them on you."

I glanced over my shoulder and smiled. "It only just now occurred to me that this wrought iron headboard would be perfect for chaining me up. But I suppose it occurred to you a long time ago."

"No. It's a total coincidence," he said with a straight face. Then he beamed at me. "Oh, and by the way." He placed the little controller on the bed and tapped it with one finger.

I arched up off the mattress as the plug in my ass started to vibrate and stimulate my pleasure spot, moaning appreciatively. "Man that feels good. What number is that?"

"Two."

"Mmmmmm." I relaxed back against the mattress and enjoyed the waves of pleasure that were pulsating through my body, my eyes sliding shut as I squeezed my butt tightly around the plug. I reached down and began stroking my cock without even thinking about it.

After a while I rolled over onto my stomach, wantonly rubbing my cock on the bed as the plug worked its magic in my ass. I reached out and caressed Dante's uninjured thigh as I said, "Right now, I'm having all the fun. What in that case is going to bring you the most pleasure?"

"Oh believe me, the sight of your sweet ass gyrating like that while you get yourself off is bringing me all sorts of pleasure."

"Is there anything in there to beat me with?"

He hesitated, then said, "There are a couple little floggers. But you know how I feel about hurting you."

I sighed and said, "You wouldn't be hurting me. You'd be getting us both off."

"Do something for me, Charlie."

"Anything."

He grinned at me. "Roll onto your back and chain yourself to the headboard."

I did as I was told, snapping one of the quite familiar cuffs on my left wrist, running the chain through the bars of the headboard, and then fastening the remaining cuff to my other wrist. Dante moaned appreciatively and ran his fingertips down my torso, then came back up to play with my nipples. He smiled at me as he tapped the remote control again.

I gasped and arched up off the bed again as the waves of pleasure magnified, each pulse inside me answered with a throb of my cock. "That feels so good," I murmured. "What number is it?"

"Four."

"Damn it! You're trying to finish me off so I'll end the discussion about getting you off!"

He was still smiling. "Maybe."

Dante tapped the remote again and I cried out, thrusting my rock hard, leaking cock into the air. He slid his fingertips down my body and between my spread legs, and stroked the soft, sensitive skin right beneath my balls. "Oh fuck," I ground out, trying to fight back my impending orgasm. "What number?"

"Five." He leaned forward, took one of my hard pink nipples between his lips, and suckled me as he caressed the underside of my balls.

"Mmmmm." I threw my head back and closed my eyes, rational thought crowded out by blinding pleasure.

He released my nipple, the cool air making it tighten and tingle since it was wet from his mouth. "And this, angel," he said, "is six." He took the tip of my cock between his lips as he tapped the remote, and the orgasm tore from my body. I yelled incoherently, my hips coming up off the bed, and Dante followed, sucking my cock as I shot into his mouth again and again, thrusting reflexively.

The orgasm was incredibly, shatteringly intense, and as I came down from it, he ran a fingertip over the remote, dialing back the vibration. He didn't turn it off, though. He left it set to a low, pleasant hum inside me, and released my cock from his mouth.

I was sweaty, shaking, and panting as he stretched out on his side, rested his head on my chest and draped an arm over me. "Holy shit," I murmured when I could speak again. He looked up at me, and I bent my head to kiss him. "That was totally unfair, I got to have all the fun. We can't keep being so one-sided when it comes to sex. We have to take this to a place that's going to make you feel good, too."

"That made me feel *incredibly* good. I loved seeing you like that, distilled down to pure sex, lost to the pleasure."

"It was still all for me."

"No, the chains were for me," he argued, and kissed my chest. My arms were still bound, stretched above my head, and neither of us were in a hurry to do anything about it. He finally turned the toy off and eased it out of my body.

"They were for both of us. I love being tied up." I felt a little tremor go through him when I said that. "Please Dante, let me get you off. I need to make you cum."

"This was a lot for our first time out after my injury. Just rest, angel. We're both tired."

I sighed and said, "I know you're just saying that to get me to drop the subject." He grinned at me. "We have to figure this out, Dante, and soon. Never climaxing again because you can't let yourself whip me is just not an option."

He was quiet for a while, his head still on my chest, his right arm in its cast slung over me. Then he said softly, "I'm sorry I'm so fucked up and only get off on inflicting pain. I don't know what the fuck is wrong with me."

"Nothing! So you have needs that aren't totally vanilla. So what? That's just how you're wired. Turns out, I'm wired to get off on receiving pain, which actually means we're perfect for each other."

"I don't want to hurt you."

"But you wouldn't be! Don't you see? The one time you spanked me, it brought me so much pleasure. That's not hurting me, it's making me feel good. It's giving me what I need!"

"You didn't even know you wanted that before you met me." He reached up and did something to one of the cuffs around my wrist, then the other. The mechanism sprang open and I rolled onto my side, taking Dante in my arms.

"Before I met you, I was a mess when it came to sex. The reason Jamie and I never got farther than oral in all those years together was totally because of me, because of my fear and my hang-ups," I told him. "It's so different with you, Dante. I stopped being afraid. Part of it has to do with the way you take charge and guide me, and a huge part of it has to do with how *totally right* this feels."

He was quiet for a while before saying, "Sometimes, I wonder what you're doing with me."

"Seriously?" He nodded, and I said, "You're perfect for me, and not just in terms of sex. You make me feel safe, and happy, and loved. You also make me feel secure, which is kind of huge, since I've always felt insecure about pretty much everything," I told him. "And it's more than how you make me feel. I love who you are. I fell for you on our first date. I fell for the guy in the expensive suit who was willing to climb over fences and pick locks and fight off smelly dogs, and keep a sense of humor throughout it. The guy who then turned around and held me while I cried."

"You had me at Hello Kitty."

I burst out laughing. "Really?"

Dante smiled at me. "No, not really. You had me the very first time you turned to face me in the bar, and I looked into those big, green eyes. You're such an incredibly beautiful boy, Charlie, with that perfect face and perfect body. I would have expected you to be cocky and arrogant, but you weren't at all. Instead, you were so sweet and humble," he said, running his fingertips over my cheek. "I could tell you were going through some stuff, because there was such sadness in your eyes. One of my very first thoughts when I looked at you was that I wanted to take that sadness away, that I would do anything to see those eyes sparkle with happiness."

"Well, you've always done an excellent job of making me happy."

"That's not true," he said. "I was enough of an ass to break up with you."

"You thought that was for my own good."

"Then I chained you to a person and left the country! Why you haven't punched me in the face for that one, I'll never know."

"You chained me to Christopher. I ended up getting a best friend out of the deal."

243

He grinned and rolled his eyes. "Everything I say, you make into a positive."

"Yup. Really happy people have a tendency to do that."

Chapter Eighteen

Three weeks later, both of Dante's casts had come off. His hands had been weak from lack of use, but Dante worked his physical therapy like a job, doing his exercises religiously, and was finally to the point where he could hold things in a closed fist with each hand. Meanwhile, I'd returned to work. Nolan's was the hot new lunch destination, apparently, and I'd been pulling in great tips.

Dante also busied himself by taking an active role in a couple of his investment properties. One was a restaurant in the Marina district. He'd completely gutted the building, and would be redecorating, hiring a new staff, and designing the menu from the ground up. I came home from work one day to find blueprints spread all over our bed. Dante sat cross-legged in the midst of them, making notes on a yellow legal pad. He had an endearing habit of wearing my clothes around the house, and was dressed in a pair of my gym shorts and an old Stanford t-shirt.

"Hi angel." His face lit up in a bright smile, and I leaned over to kiss him.

"Hi sweetheart. Whatcha doing?"

"I got the revised blueprints for the restaurant today, so I'm doing a little fine-tuning."

I tilted my head to look at the big sheets of paper. "I can barely make sense of them."

"I've always been fascinated by blueprints," he told me. "In another life, I would have loved to study architecture."

"Why not in this life?"

"Well, you know," he said, setting the legal pad aside. "I went into the family business right out of high school. College is for people without eight generations of tradition resting on their shoulders."

"So now that you're retired, why not go back to school and pursue a degree in architecture?"

"That'd be kind of awkward, wouldn't it? Going back to school at twenty-nine? I'd be the oldest one in all my classes."

"So?"

"I don't know. It'd be weird."

"No it wouldn't. To start with, why don't you just try a course or two though U.C. extension? See if architecture really is where your passion lies."

"That's actually a good idea. The students would probably be closer to my age there, too." Dante gathered up the blueprints and set them on the floor beside the bed, and I climbed onto the mattress and straddled his lap, kissing him.

"What about you, Charlie? You ever think about going back to school?" he asked when we broke apart, looking up at me as he linked his fingers at the back of my neck.

"Nah. All I ever wanted to do was play pro football. When that dream died, there was nothing else I was interested in."

"Why not take a few classes? See if anything grabs you?"

"I dunno. I was never much of a student. I think that even if I hadn't gotten injured and had to drop out, I probably would have flunked out of Stanford anyway," I said.

"I think we should take a few classes together through university extension. We both might discover our passion."

"Oh, I already discovered my passion. Weeks ago," I said with a grin, and kissed him deeply. He tugged my t-shirt out of my jeans, and then pulled it off over my head and tossed it away from us.

In a move that showed me exactly how much he'd healed, he slid off the bed and stood up with me wrapped around him, my arms around his neck, legs around his waist as he cupped my ass. He held me like that for a long moment, kissing me, claiming my mouth with his tongue, and then laid me on my back on the mattress and continued undressing me. "You're obviously feeling better," I said happily.

"I am. The hands are both working, and my leg's not giving me problems. In fact, I felt so good today that I went out and did some shopping."

"Oh yeah? Where'd you go?"

He reached under the bed and pulled out a small brown paper bag, which he placed on my bare stomach. "Hardware store."

I peeked inside the bag and beamed at him, then pulled out the bundle of white rope and turned it over in my hands. "Does this mean what I think it means?"

"I've been thinking about this for weeks," he said, sliding his hands up my bare thighs. "I tried to convince myself I could do without, that maybe I could somehow get past my kinks. But no matter how hard I tried to convince myself, I just couldn't. I really do need this, Charlie. I don't know why I do, but it's a part of me."

"And that's fine with me! More than fine. I want it too. I *need* it! Just like you do."

He sat beside me on the mattress. "I want to believe you. I want to believe you're not just going along with this because it's what I want."

"I *crave* this. Ever since the first time you spanked me, I've longed for it. God, just the thought of it makes me throb. It makes me want to drop to my knees and beg you for it." I picked up his hand and placed it on my hard cock.

He stroked my cock gently, then said, "I'm afraid of going too far and really hurting you. If I do something that's too painful or that you don't like, do you promise to tell me?"

"Of course. You need to trust me, Dante, just like I trust you. I'll tell you if it gets to be too much. You won't really hurt me, because I won't let you," I told him.

Dante was quiet for a while. Finally he looked me in the eye. "As long as it remains enjoyable for you, and as long as you promise to tell me to stop if it becomes too much, I want us to do this."

"I'm so glad," I said drawing him into a hug. "And it's going to be so good. I promise."

"It's kind of funny that you're the one reassuring me. You've never been fucked before. I should be doing the reassuring."

"I don't need reassuring. I just need you in me."

He smiled at that. Then he opened the nightstand and pulled out a sheet of paper, which he handed to me. "I didn't know how to work this into the conversation sooner," he said, "but a couple weeks ago when I was at a check-up at my doctor's office, I asked him to do a blood test. I'd always been careful, but I wanted to be one hundred percent certain that I was safe. Turns out I am. So I wanted to ask your permission to fuck you without any barriers between us."

I reached across him and tossed the medical report back in the nightstand. "Absolutely."

My amusement must have shown on my face, because he raised an eyebrow at me and said, "What?"

"Nothing. It's just cute. You had a whole speech prepared, kind of like you were conducting a business meeting. You even had paperwork, a visual aid."

He grinned at me. "I've never negotiated a safe sex agreement. But then, I've never been in a committed relationship, either. It's new territory."

"Okay," I said, "meeting adjourned. Now back to the incredibly exciting item in my hand." I held the rope up and waved it.

Dante exhaled softly and took the rope from me, uncoiling the end that held it all together in a neat bundle. "I've dreamt about this," he admitted quietly.

"Me too."

"This is actually my tool of choice, by the way. I love using rope. There's something very sensual about it, I think."

"What do I do?"

"Just relax and hopefully, enjoy the process. It's going to take me about half an hour to fully bind you. It should feel very snug, but it shouldn't hurt, so let me know if anything's too tight. Any time you want me to stop for any reason, just tell me and we'll stop immediately. Okay?"

"Okay."

Dante instructed me to get up on my knees on the edge of the mattress, and then he went to work. Patiently, meticulously, he wound the rope around my torso, knotting it in the center of my chest, running it under my arms, across my back, over my shoulders. After a while, I stopped trying to analyze the pattern and just closed my eyes and relaxed while he worked on me.

My arms were bent behind my back, hands holding elbows, bound in place, and then he picked me up and laid me on my back and bound my legs, knees bent back to my shoulders, legs spread, ass tilted upward. Being put in that position sent a tremor of desire through me, and my breathing picked up as my cock pressed against my stomach and throbbed in anticipation.

Eventually, Dante stepped back and asked, "How does that feel?"

I considered the question, raising my head to look down at myself. I was bound very securely, the only thing I could move was my head. The rope wasn't just tied to do a job, it was tied decoratively, intricate loops and knots and cross-overs highlighting my body. It was more than erotic, it was surprisingly artistic. Beautiful. And it felt so incredibly good. It felt secure. "I feel like you're holding me in your arms."

He smiled and said, "That's exactly what it's supposed to feel like."

He stripped himself, grabbed the briefcase from the closet and climbed up beside me, kissing me while he caressed my body. When he sat back to get something from the case, I saw that his thick, impressive cock was jutting out, its tip glistening tantalizingly. My mouth actually watered at the sight of that, and I whispered, "Please sir, can I taste your precum?"

The 'sir' came completely naturally, practically of its own volition. It just seemed to go with submitting to him. He paused and looked at me, then got up on his knees beside me. I opened my mouth and stuck my tongue out for him, and he took his cock in his hand and slowly ran the moist tip down the length of my tongue. I actually trembled with pleasure, and savored his taste before swallowing. "Thank you sir," I murmured, and he smiled fondly at me.

He moved down to my ass and lubed my hole before pushing a finger into me. He'd fingered me several times over the last three weeks, and had even worked progressively larger toys into me. But I still didn't get how his big, thick cock was ever going to fit in me. Instead of worrying about it though, I just concentrated on relaxing and opening myself up to him. After a while, he worked a second finger into me. When he crooked his finger and hit my pleasure spot, I let out a long, low moan.

"I'm going to add a third finger, angel," he told me, and pushed it in me with the first two. As he finger fucked me, he explained, "I'm going to work you open as much as possible and then put a toy in you while I whip you. That way I can pull it out and mount you as soon as I'm ready."

"Oh God yes," I moaned, my eyes sliding shut, a shudder of desire going through me as my head rolled back.

He fingered me thoroughly before working more lube into me, followed by a thick dildo. It was the biggest thing I'd ever had in me, and he pushed it in slowly but steadily, his palm against its flat base. I gasped and squirmed a little, and his free hand took hold of my cock, pumping it slowly as the toy stretched me, readied me.

Finally, he told me, "You did it, angel. You took all of it." I smiled and let out my breath, and he climbed up beside me and kissed me, deeply, tenderly, fondling my cock, the dildo completely filling my ass. "You're doing great, Charlie," he told me, smiling and brushing my sweat dampened hair from my forehead.

"I want you in me so bad." My voice was a bit rough, my breath fast and shallow.

"Soon, angel. Very soon." He took something from the case and ran it up my cock, and I tilted my head up to see the black leather crop in his hand. "I'm going to whip you now Charlie, if you're absolutely sure this is what you want."

"I need it. Please, sir. Beat me and fuck me. Please," I begged, my cock throbbing as my entire body quivered with anticipation.

He rolled me onto my knees, my ass sticking up in the air, legs tucked underneath me, and dragged me to the edge of the mattress. God I loved being manhandled like that. The big dildo slid out of my ass just a bit, and he took hold of the end of it and fucked me with it a few times before nestling it deep inside me again. He picked up the lube and squirted some onto his hand, and worked his shaft for a few moments, prepping himself, getting ready for the moment when he would finally, *finally* be inside me. I shook and moaned at the thought of it.

I felt him running the crop over my ass, almost petting me with it. "Remember, you can stop this at any time," he said. "One word is all it takes. You say stop, we stop."

"Please," I begged, "please. Make me yours." I didn't even know where that came from, but it was exactly right. He was about to lay claim to me, totally, irrevocably. I would belong to him after this, heart and soul, mind and body. I wanted it more than I'd ever wanted anything in my entire life.

He slid the crop down between my legs and stroked my balls with it, driving me wild with desire. I begged him to whip me, and finally, the first delicious blow fell across my exposed ass. I yelled as sensation exploded through my body. It was intense and it hurt like hell and it was absolutely, unequivocally wonderful.

He brought the whip down again and again, and I surrendered completely to the sharp, stinging pain that made my cock jump and throb and leak precum all over the bed. Primal yells tore from me, animalistic, guttural. All rational thought was suspended, leaving only raw sex and pleasure/pain and Dante and me. Nothing else mattered, nothing but this, right now, the two of us giving and taking exactly what we both needed.

When the whipping stopped I cried out and begged for more, wildly, desperately. But then Dante pulled the big toy from my ass, and I felt him position his cock at my stretched little opening. "Oh God yes, please, fuck me Dante," I begged shamelessly.

He took hold of my hips and pushed against my hole, and the head of his cock slipped inside me suddenly. I gasped and tensed up, and he whispered to me soothingly, reassuring me as he held perfectly still and let me get used to the feeling of him inside me. Then slowly, he eased his cock into me.

It was an incredibly tight fit, he was much thicker than the dildo. When he was only halfway in, I whimpered and struggled a little. I didn't know how I'd take any more of that huge cock, I was already so full. Dante withdrew a couple inches, and stroked my back as he said softly, "You're doing great, angel." He held still for a moment before again slowly sinking into me, and I breathed deeply and let myself relax, reassured by the knowledge that he was taking care of me.

He began thrusting, being careful not to go too deep, sliding only a few inches of his cock in and out of me, and I relaxed underneath him even more, allowing more of him inside me. He started going deeper as he felt me open up. When he grazed the pleasure spot inside me, I cried out in ecstasy and relaxed even more. Soon I was begging him to take me harder.

Dante started pumping in and out of me forcefully, claiming me, and I moaned loudly as he reached under me and began stroking my cock. "Yes. God yes, fuck me Dante," I yelled, and his thrusts got harder still.

He was absolutely pounding me by that point, slamming into me up to his balls, which slapped against my body with each thrust. It was wild and intense and perfect, and I totally gave myself over to it. "You're mine," he growled as he took me.

"Yes. Yours. All of me," I told him, each sentence a gasp as my body absorbed the force of his thrusts.

Dante cried out and shoved his cock in me as far as it would go, and his entire body shuddered as his cum shot deep into me. That triggered my orgasm, and I yelled as I shot my load all over the bed and up onto my bound, naked body, spurt after spurt, as Dante thrust into me again and again and again.

Finally, he dropped down on top of me for a moment, his body shaking, then pulled out of me and rolled me onto my back. He kissed me forcefully, and I parted my lips for him. When he broke the kiss, he looked deep into my eyes and told me, softly this time, "You're mine."

A tremor of pleasure coursed through me, my voice rough from yelling as I replied, "Yes. Yours. And you're mine." He smiled and kissed me again as an aftershock made my body tremble.

He brushed my hair from my face and told me softly, "I adore you, Charlie. I'll spend the rest of my life loving you, cherishing you and taking care of you."

I smiled at him and whispered, "I'll do the same for you."

Dante unwound the ropes quickly and efficiently, then massaged feeling back into my arms and legs. He led me to the bathroom, where he filled the tub and climbed in with me. I sat between his legs and leaned against his chest as he gently soaped me and rinsed me off. "How do you feel?" he asked.

"Well fucked." I grinned broadly.

"So…was that really okay?"

"It was so much better than okay. It was absolutely perfect."

Chapter Nineteen

Two weeks earlier, I'd said to Christopher, "Bad news. I've decided that you and I are family, and as family, you're required to spend Thanksgiving with me."

"Why is that bad news?" he'd wanted to know.

"Because I'm spending it with the Dombruso clan, and that means you are, too."

As we pulled up in front of Mrs. Dombruso's palatial Pacific Heights mansion on Thanksgiving Day, Christopher was wide-eyed and clearly nervous. He was wearing his best outfit, a black button down shirt and black dress pants, and it made him look thinner and even more fragile than usual. I put my arm around his shoulders and squeezed him reassuringly as I said, "I don't know about you, but I'm scared shitless."

"I don't belong here," he said in a small voice. "I agreed to come because it totally sucks to be alone on Thanksgiving. But this is worse. I'm an outsider. They won't want me here."

Dante said, "I want you here, and Nana wants you here. We're the only two who actually get a vote, by the way. But besides that, everyone's going to love you. My family...well, a couple of them are assholes, but every family's like that. The rest of them are good people, and they'll welcome both of you with open arms. Just wait and see."

"Charlie belongs here, I don't," Christopher insisted softly.

"You're my family, Christopher Robin," I told him. "So of course you belong here. Family belongs together on Thanksgiving."

He took a deep breath and looked at me for a long moment. Finally, he said, "Well…shit. Okay."

I beamed at him. "Let's do this thing."

Dante led the way into the grand Queen Anne Victorian. Inside was total and complete chaos. Kids ran around chasing each other and screaming. A Golden Retriever ran by with a mangled doll between its teeth. Two women were having an argument in the living room, and a group of men were talking and laughing loudly in the parlor to our right.

One of the men noticed us and exclaimed, "Hey, there they are!" He strode into the foyer and kissed Dante on both cheeks.

"This is my brother Mikey," Dante said to us. "Mikey, this is my boyfriend Charlie and our friend Christopher."

His brother rolled his eyes. "To the rest of the world I'm Mike. To my family, I'm forever Mikey." He shook my hand and then Christopher's as he said, "Pleasure to meet you both. Nana's been asking for you, Charlie. She's in the kitchen terrorizing the cooks, maybe you can go and placate her. Just watch out for flying chef's knives."

I hoped he was kidding. Dante put his arm around my waist and I took Christopher's hand. We wound through the crowd, Dante calling greetings along the way and promising to come right back after we saw Mrs. Dombruso.

The huge kitchen was even more chaotic than the rest of the house. At least a dozen uniformed cooks and wait staff were bustling around, preparing what looked like enough food for the entire city of San Francisco. Not only was every traditional Thanksgiving food being prepared, but so were a bunch of Italian dishes and maybe two dozen desserts.

Mrs. Dombruso was rolling around in what looked like an electric office chair, barking orders and tasting dishes. Her white hair was piled in a giant up-do that would have done Marie Antoinette proud, and she was wearing a dark orange velvet gown and loads of jewelry, her glasses on her lap. When she caught sight of us she exclaimed, "Finally! Fashionably late doesn't apply to family functions, boys."

Dante kissed both her cheeks and said, "Sorry, Nana." We were maybe five minutes past the designated start time, but everyone else had apparently known to get there early.

When he straightened up and stepped back, Mrs. Dombruso stared at Christopher and me and demanded, "Well?"

It took me a moment to realize what she wanted, and then I too stepped forward and kissed her, followed by Christopher. She smiled happily at that. "Such good boys. All three of you. You know how to treat your old Nana." Then she said, "So, Charlie, I don't know what traditions your family had as Irish Americans. I told the cooks to be prepared to make you anything you normally have for Thanksgiving once you arrived."

"I don't need anything special, Mrs. Dombruso. This all looks wonderful." Thanksgiving had always meant my parents and me and Uncle Al and his family, gathered around a dry turkey and jellied cranberry sauce in the shape of a can. I felt a pang of sadness at the thought of my family, and wondered what my father was doing that day. I hoped he'd gone to his brother Al's house, and wasn't spending the day alone.

She sighed and knit her brows. "I thought I told you to call me Nana." She shot Christopher a look. "You too, kiddo. I don't want any of that Mrs. Dombruso crap around here. Got it?"

"Yes ma'am," we both said in unison.

"And as for you, Christopher Robin," she'd latched on to his full name when I'd called him that in front of her once, and now went out of her way to use it, "I don't know what your heritage is or what traditions you're used to."

He was a little thrown by the question. "I have no Thanksgiving traditions to speak of, aside from watchin' football." He and I had set the DVR to record every game that was happening that day, and we had a big football marathon planned when we got home.

She thought of something, and said, "Christopher Robin, come talk to me for a moment." Nana took his hand and rolled off to a quiet corner of the kitchen, where he leaned close to talk to her.

Dante took the opportunity to pull me into his arms. "How bad is it so far?" he whispered against my ear.

"Not bad at all," I told him, sliding my hands under his unbuttoned suit jacket and holding him to me. He felt warm and strong and solid in my arms.

"What the fuck, Dante?" a woman's voice behind us exclaimed. "Did you think you two had to hide in the kitchen? That your family's a bunch of fucking homophobic assholes and we're all going to keel the fuck over if we see you and your lover hugging?"

He laughed at that, and turned to the big haired busty redhead who'd just come into the kitchen. "Hardly. We were summoned by Nana. Charlie, this is my foul-mouthed cousin Melanie. Melanie, Charlie."

"Foul-mouthed? Fuck you, Dante," she said. She winked at me and took my hand. "Hiya Charlie. Welcome to the family. I apologize in advance for every crude, vulgar, politically incorrect, or flat-out insulting thing you hear over the course of this evening. Not from me, mind you, but from everyone else. I'm the well-behaved one of the bunch." She smiled at me cheerfully, then snatched a couple olives out of a glass dish and told me, "Hurry up and get your ass out there. Everyone's dying to meet you." Then she disappeared through the kitchen doorway.

"What did I get myself into?" I asked with a grin as I took Dante in my arms again.

Christopher came up to us, pulling open a packet of his orange-colored crackers. "Nana totally gets it," he said with a pleased little smile. "She noticed my food thing and promised not to try to fix me. At least, not today." He popped a cracker in his mouth.

Dinner was loud and raucous and absolutely hilarious. The more everyone drank, the louder and funnier it got. There were at least fifty or sixty family members seated at several long tables in what at one time had been a formal ballroom. Dante was the undisputed leader of the clan (well, after his grandmother), and his family obviously loved and respected him. But they still felt free to tease him mercilessly at every opportunity.

Christopher and I were both accepted as part of the family without hesitation, which pretty much blew me away. This was so wildly, refreshingly different from my own family. And thank God for that. Christopher remained quiet throughout the meal, but he was smiling and watching the proceedings with a sparkle in his blue eyes, taking it all in. We sat side-by-side, so close our arms were touching. At one point he leaned over and whispered in my ear, "I'm having the best time. Thank you for inviting me."

"Thank you for saying yes," I whispered back.

Later on things quieted down a bit, everyone lulled by the mountains of rich food. The adults retired to the living room, and the kids were rounded up by the teenagers and taken to watch cartoons in the in-house theater.

I was happy and relaxed, holding Dante's hand with Christopher at my side. Then Dante cleared his throat and stood up, saying, "Could I have everyone's attention, please?"

All eyes were on him as he grinned at me and cleared his throat again. He was nervous about something. Nana exclaimed, "Oh shit, you're doing this now?" She shoved her glasses onto her face, grabbed a little camcorder that was on the seat beside her, and pushed the on-button. She pointed the camera at us, flashed a thumbs-up, and said, "Okay, go ahead."

Dante laughed at that, then got down on one knee and took my hand. "Angel, I love you more than anything. I love you more than I ever knew it was possible to love someone. You're my life, you're everything to me." He paused, his dark eyes locked with mine, and then he said softly, "Charlie Connolly, will you do me the honor of being my husband?"

I gasped and stammered, "Yes. God yes! Of course."

I had no idea what his family's reaction was. They could have cheered, they could have gasped and fainted, I really didn't notice, because all my attention was on the beautiful man before me. Dante grabbed me in a hug and whispered, "Thank you, angel. You've made me so incredibly happy," and kissed me, deeply and passionately, right in front of everyone.

When Dante finally released me, Christopher grabbed me in a hug. "Congratulations, Charlie," he said, and kissed my cheek. I was dragged to my feet then and passed around in an onslaught of hugs and kisses and back-slaps. Nana finally caught my hand and pulled me down into a big hug, and said, "You were already a part of the family, Charlie. This just makes it official." She kept hold of my hand as she turned to Dante and said, "So, is a gay homosexual wedding the same as a straight one? Is one of you wearing white? Do we do a bridal shower, or is that insulting? I'll call tomorrow and reserve the Mark Hopkins for New Year's Eve. That's a nice time for a wedding, don't you think?"

"That's in just a few weeks, Nana," Dante said, coming up to us and slipping his arm around my waist. "We need more time to plan."

"Like hell you do. What do you want, to wait until I'm dead and then get married? Fuck that. You can get married on New Year's. I'll take care of everything, and it'll be perfectly romantic, you'll see." She craned her neck and called, "Christopher Robin, where are you? Come here, son."

He wove his way through the crowd, and she took his hand. "So this little cupcake is going to be, what, the best man? Is there still a best man in a gay wedding? Well, sure, why wouldn't there be?" she said, answering her own question. "And of course that's you."

"I...I really don't know," Christopher said.

"Oh that's definitely you," I told him with a big smile. "Though I guess I should ask you officially. Christopher Robin, will you be my best man?"

He grinned shyly and said, "Sure. Thanks for asking me."

Nana barreled ahead with, "So, Christopher Robin, I'm going to need your help. I need your artistic eye with this whole event, to make sure it's perfect for my favorite grandson." She caught Mikey's eye and yelled, "That's right, he's my favorite! So what? You're my second favorite. Deal with it!"

*****

A couple hours later, Dante took my hand and pulled me into a second floor bedroom, then pinned me to the wall and kissed me. "Hi," he said with a grin when we finally came up for air.

"Hi." I beamed at him.

"We're getting married," he murmured, resting his forehead against mine.

"Mmhmm. Really soon, apparently."

"I can try to talk Nana out of New Year's if you want. I know that gives us very little time to plan."

"No, let her have her fun. I can't wait to be your husband, so the sooner the better as far as I'm concerned."

He kissed me again before asking, "Did you totally hate the fact that I asked you to marry me in front of my whole family? I know PDA isn't your favorite thing, and maybe I shouldn't have—"

I cut him off with a kiss and said, "It was wonderful. I can't believe you went down on one knee and everything."

He smiled at me. "I wanted to do it right. I'm only getting married once, after all, so no cutting corners." He took my hand, led me to the twin bed and pulled me onto his lap.

I looked around the little bedroom, "Where exactly have you brought me?"

"My room. I mean, the room I lived in as a kid. I moved in with Nana when I was seven, after…."

I cupped his cheek and nodded in understanding. Then I lightened the mood by saying, "So, you snuck your boyfriend into your bedroom under your grandmother's nose. Shame on you."

"My fiancé," he corrected.

I smiled widely and said, "Yes. Your fiancé. We'd better say that a whole bunch in the next few weeks, since this is going to be one short engagement."

"You know, while you were nursing me back to health, I promised to take you somewhere warm and tropical. Fiji, I think I said. Would you like to make that our honeymoon destination?"

"I'm fine with anything, just as long as it's really private. I want to spend the entire honeymoon tied to our bed with your cock buried in my ass."

He grinned and shook his head. "My insatiable little angel." We'd had many intense, wonderful, mind-blowing encounters since that first one. Every time our roommate left the apartment, I dragged Dante to the bedroom or got dragged there in turn. The thought of a private location where we could be alone and fuck like bunnies made my cock hard.

Dante noticed that right away, and grinned wickedly. He sat me on the mattress and dropped to his knees between my legs. As he tugged down the zipper of my khakis, I exclaimed, "Oh my God! Dante, what are you doing? Your entire family's downstairs! We can't!" I bit back a moan as his warm, wet mouth surrounded my cock. He sucked me urgently, his dark eyes locked with mine. I pressed a hand to my mouth to stop myself from crying out as I came violently minutes later, reflexively thrusting as he swallowed my load.

Once he'd sucked me dry, he slid his mouth off my cock, tucked me in again and zipped me up. "What was that?" I asked with a grin as he took my hand and pulled me to my feet.

Dante winked at me and slapped my ass. "Dessert."

Chapter Twenty

"I know y'all totally snuck off and had sex yesterday during Thanksgiving at Nana's, and left me stuck chattin' up Cousin Rachael. Who bah the way, is a total and complete cougah." We were in our living room and Christopher's hands were on his narrow hips, the big leather falconry gloves riding up to his elbows as he raised an eyebrow at me. "She tried to lure me into the pantry with her. Is that where y'all were? Diddlin' with the dry goods?" He and Dante were in the middle of one of their Peaches training sessions, and Christopher was so flustered by the dog that he forgot to hold his accent in check.

"No, of course not," I said.

He dumped a gluten-free dog biscuit into his hand from the box on the table. "Peaches, sit," he said, showing the dog the biscuit. Peaches curled back his lips, displayed his underbite and let out a high-pitched growl. In response, Dante shot him with a squirt bottle, and Christopher exclaimed, "No, Peaches!"

"We were only gone a few minutes," I told him, standing on the coffee table with my arms crossed over my chest, out of range in case Peaches went ballistic and tried to kill everyone.

"So just a blowjob then?" he asked, turning toward me again. I guess I looked guilty, because he rolled his eyes and said, "I knew it." Peaches started to lunge at him when Christopher's back was turned, so Dante squirted him again. The dog stopped his attack and shook himself.

"You two should give up on this," I said. "Peaches is uncivilizable."

"No way," said Dante. "I'm finally getting to shoot that little shit." He twirled the squirt bottle around his index finger and grinned at me, and I rolled my eyes.

Christopher rubbed his nose with the back of his gloved hand and said, "I think I am giving up for now. I can only take so many attempts on my life in one day. We'll give it another go tomorrow." He pulled the gloves off and tucked them under his arm.

"I need pie after that," Dante said, handing the squirt bottle to Christopher. "Cover me." He headed for the kitchen, where our refrigerator was crammed full of the leftovers Nana had forced on us yesterday. The dog nipped at his heels and Christopher chased after them, yelling, "No, Peaches!" and squirting him the whole way.

Someone knocked on the door as I was jumping off the table. I crossed the room and swung the door open, and went full on deer-in-headlights.

"Charlie," my father said by way of greeting, shifting uncomfortably from foot to foot.

"What are you doing here?"

"I just, you know, thought I should bring you your mail." He thrust a few envelopes at me, and I took them hesitantly. I saw at a glance they were all just junk mail. "Mind if I come in?"

I stepped back and let my father into my apartment, and he came in and sank down awkwardly on the edge of the sofa. I perched on a chair on the other side of the coffee table and studied him warily.

It looked like my father had aged twenty years in the past few weeks. His complexion was pale and there were dark circles under his eyes. He wore an old, beat-up coat that my mother used to complain about with a stained t-shirt underneath, and it looked like he hadn't shaved in a week. Bachelorhood was most definitely not agreeing with Walter Connolly.

"So...some things were said," he began, looking at his big hands, which were clutched on his lap. "I was angry. And confused. I didn't know how to deal with...well, you know."

"The fact that I'm gay."

"Yeah. That." He paused and scratched his cheek, not meeting my gaze. Then he said, "I know I messed up, Charlie. You're my kid. I shouldn't have kicked you out of the house. That was wrong. So I wanted to tell you that, if you wanna come back home, the door's open to you."

"No thank you," I said quietly.

He looked up at me. "It won't be like before. Your mother left me, I'm not sure if you knew that. I've had a lot of time to think since she's been gone. I'm not angry anymore, Charlie."

"This is my home now."

My father looked around, as if he'd failed to notice the apartment before. "Oh. Well, this is a real nice place. Used to be Jamie's, right? I remember it. Only, it's fancier now." He was looking at the big TV when he said that. "Jamie don't live here anymore, does he?"

"No, he and his husband live in the Richmond now, by their place of business." I'd said that for shock value, just to see how my dad would react.

He did pretty well. He knit his brows and really tried to take it in stride as he said, "Oh. So Jamie's...."

"Also gay. He was my boyfriend for years." I was pushing him, I knew that. I wanted to goad a reaction out of him. I didn't trust this kinder, gentler Walter and wanted him to expose himself as the homophobe that he was.

But all my father said was, "Oh. I never knew that." He blinked repeatedly as he tried to process that information.

"Well no, of course not. I could never tell you, because I knew how you'd react if you ever found out I was gay." I knit my brows and said, "Turns out, I was exactly right."

"I'm sorry I reacted the way I did." It was the first time I'd ever heard him apologize to anyone for any reason. "I messed up. It really caught me off guard. I know I reacted badly, and I want to make amends."

"I think it's too late for that."

He wasn't done trying, though. I realized all of a sudden that our entire relationship had shifted. I didn't need him anymore, but he needed me. He was a mess and probably really lonely since my mother left him. That was why he was here. It was a weird concept, the idea of my father actually needing me.

He said, "Charlie, I don't blame you for being angry. I was an asshole. The worst kind of father, one who turns on his own kid."

"Pretty much," I muttered.

"C'mon. Give your old dad another chance. What do you say?"

I had lived my whole life trying to please my father. I'd always felt that his love was something that needed to be earned, not something given unconditionally. All I'd ever wanted was for him to love me and be proud of me. It was why I pushed myself to excel in football, his favorite sport. It was why I'd tried hard in school, and why I went to work for my uncle and his awful exterminator business. It was a big part of the reason why I'd tried to deny my sexuality, why I stayed in the closet so long, why I'd tried to make myself marry Callie.

But then the thing I'd always feared so much actually happened. I lost my father's love and got kicked out of my home. And I not only survived it, I ended up thriving. It turned out I was so much stronger than I ever realized.

I studied the man before me carefully. I'd always been afraid of my father. He used to tower over me, he seemed big as a house when I was little. When he yelled, it used to fill me with terror. Apparently some part of me had continued to see him that way right into adulthood, as this huge, scary hulk. But when I looked at him now, really looked at him, he was just an old man in worn out clothes who looked like he needed a long nap and a good meal. Despite myself, I felt sorry for him. Unexpectedly, I found myself letting go of a lot of that hurt and anger, and actually forgiving him. I could love my father unconditionally, even if he hadn't been man enough to do the same for me.

"What you did to me wasn't okay," I said quietly. "But I love you, Dad. I always will, no matter what. I'm obviously not going to move back home, I'm a grown man and I stayed too long as it was. But if you want to try to be a part of my new life, well, I guess we could figure out how to make that work."

"Yeah, okay." His chin trembled for just a moment, and his eyes got a little moist. But he didn't cry. It wasn't something he was capable of.

This wasn't going to be a big hug-it-out moment. That was another thing my father couldn't do. I stood up and said, "Come into the kitchen. There are a couple people I'd like you to meet." Okay, so maybe that was one last test, and obviously, he had to pass it if he was really going to be a part of my life.

Christopher was sitting on the kitchen counter, watching us closely when we came in. Of course he'd heard everything in this small apartment. Dante was leaning against the opposite counter with his big arms crossed over his chest, muscles bulging in his tight t-shirt. There was a dark expression on his face, and his eyes were blazing. I'd never seen Dante like that, in what must be full mob boss mode. Oh man, was it sexy! I had to fight back a grin.

"Dad," I said, "this is my best friend Christopher." My roommate held up a hand by way of greeting. "And this," I said, coming up to Dante and resting my hand on his big bicep, "is my fiancé, Dante Dombruso."

"Holy shit," my father muttered. It occurred to me that maybe my Teamster father knew about organized crime in this city. Maybe he knew exactly who was staring him down and bringing to life the expression 'if looks could kill'.

Dante pushed off the counter and came to stand right in front of my dad, arms still crossed over his chest. He was intimidating as hell when he wanted to be, and God was it hot. "You hurt Charlie. You hurt the person who means more to me than anyone else in this world," Dante told him in a low voice. "You do that again, and it'll be the last thing you ever do."

A burst of laughter escaped me, and I pressed my knuckles to my mouth and tried to cover it by clearing my throat. Everyone in the room turned to stare at me, and I said, "Damn. I've never seen you in action, Dante. That's impressive." I smiled at him, and he raised an eyebrow at me. "But you don't have to threaten my dad. He knows he messed up. I'm done letting him hurt me, he doesn't have that kind of power over me anymore. So, instead of threatening to chuck him in the bay after fitting him with a set of cement loafers, how about if you just shake hands with your future father-in-law?" Dante grinned, just a little, and then got serious again as he turned back to my dad and stuck his hand out. My dad shook it quickly.

A slightly hysterical yip came from the end of the kitchen. Peaches was in his pen, vibrating with excitement, wagging his stumpy tail so hard that the back three-quarters of the dog was wagging along with it. "Peaches!" My father rushed to the pen and snatched up the dog. Instead of trying to chew my father's head off, the dog barked delightedly and licked his face.

"You have *got* to be kidding me," Christopher murmured.

"I never thought I'd see this little fella again," my father said happily. "I thought your mother took him along to Ohio. How did he get here?"

"She dropped him off on the way to the airport. She didn't want to leave him at home with you, because she thought you'd take him to the pound," I told him.

"I would never do that, not in a million years. Why would I?"

I shrugged and said, "Guess she was mistaken. Do you want to take him with you? He'd enjoy being back in his home and his yard. He doesn't like apartment life." Or any of us.

A few minutes later, Peaches the dog went home with my dad, and Dante, Christopher and I let out a collective sigh of relief. My father and I agreed to talk soon and maybe get together to watch a game. Football had always been our common ground.

"So," I said, falling back onto the couch, "my dad was happier to see the dog than he was to see me. And my mother had a much harder time saying goodbye to the dog than her own son. I think I'm developing an inferiority complex to a smelly zombie lap dog."

"It's kind of surprising that you're as normal as you are, with those parents," Christopher told me with a little grin, curling up on a chair.

"Cement loafers?" Dante said, coming into the room and sitting beside me. "Really?"

"Well, what do you want? I was never in the mafia. I don't know a bunch of cool gangster euphemisms for offing someone," I told him with a smile.

Dante was holding a plate of pumpkin pie and fed me a forkful, his dark eyes going even darker when I ended up with whipped cream on my mouth. He leaned in and slowly licked it off my lips, and Christopher sighed and said, "Man, anything will set you two off. I'll go for a walk or something."

He started to get up, but Dante said, "No, stay. There's someplace I'm planning to take Charlie, so I'm not getting anything started."

When we finished eating, we got in Dante's BMW. It was a glorious fall day, the sky a cloudless blue, and I rested my hand on my fiancé's knee as we drove across town.

His phone rang and I picked it up and put it on speaker. "Dante? You better not have me on a fucking speaker phone," Mrs. Dombruso exclaimed.

"Hi Nana," I said, "we're in the car. This way we can both talk to you at once."

"Well, I guess that's okay then. So listen, I just got off the phone with the Mark Hopkins. The bastards are totally booked for New Year's. So then I had a flash of inspiration. We should have your wedding here, in my house! I mean, what's the point in having a grand ballroom if nobody ever gets married in it?"

Dante looked at me, and I nodded. So he said, "Sure Nana, that's a great idea."

"Tell Christopher Robin to come over this weekend. I want him to help me transform that space. He's got that, you know. Artistic eye."

"Yes ma'am," I said.

"Charlie, I'm going to need your guest list ASAP. We need to get invitations out in a hurry."

"I'm only going to have about five friends there," I told her. I tried to imagine my father attending my wedding. I'd invite him, but kind of doubted that was something he'd be able to handle. "I can probably just tell them when and where to show up."

"Nonsense! Whoever heard of a wedding without formal invitations? We aren't hobos, for Christ's sake."

I held back a laugh and agreed to get her my guest list right away.

Chapter Twenty-One

We pulled up in front of a big, white building in the Marina district right about the time Nana got off the phone with us, and I exclaimed, "Is this your new restaurant?"

"It will be. Come and take a look inside." As he unlocked the huge glass door, he said, "You have to use your imagination once we get in here. I had all the walls torn back to the studs so the entire building could be earthquake-reinforced with a new steel skeleton. The construction crew is still in the process of putting it all back together."

The main body of the restaurant was spacious, with high ceilings and lots of natural light coming through tall, leaded glass windows. The building dated from the 1920s, and Dante explained that he wanted to recreate a speakeasy feel. He showed me where the dining room would go, and the position of the bar, and said, "I've asked Christopher to paint a mural for me all along that wall over there. He's intimidated by the project, but I think he'll agree to do it."

When he took me back to where the kitchen would be he really became animated, talking about equipment and how it should all be laid out and this, that, and the other thing. I grinned and said, "Forget architecture. You should go to culinary school and become chef-owner of this place."

"I don't know about that. But I am looking forward to putting the menu together. I know I want to serve Nana's pasta with marinara. And since pizza's your favorite food, I'm planning to put in a brick pizza oven."

"So, you're going Italian. That'll be good. What's the restaurant going to be called, anyway?"

"It won't be strictly Italian, I want an eclectic menu. As for the name, I'll show you," he said, leading me to the back of the building. "I hired a local metal artist to make the sign that'll go over the front door. I was shocked that she got it done already." He pulled back the flaps of a flat cardboard box that was maybe six feet long and three feet high. Inside was a bronze rectangle with the name of the restaurant spelled out in elegant raised script. It said *Charlie Connolly*.

"You're kidding," I said with a big smile. "You named it after me? And gave it both my first and last name?"

"I didn't want to be presumptuous and name it *Charlie's*. I don't know if you're going to want to have anything to do with this place. So this way, it's named in honor of you, and you can take it or leave it. But if you're interested, I really hope you'll help me run it. I'm sick of you working for your ex-boyfriend. I'm planning to be really hands-on with this restaurant, and I hope you'll work at my side."

"I'd love to, and I'm honored that you gave it my name."

He kissed me and said, "I have more to show you." He took my hand and led me to a back staircase, and when we got to the second floor, he said, "There are two apartment units on this level. I want to give one to Christopher in exchange for painting the mural. I'm still thinking about how to offer that to him without making it sound in any way, shape or form like charity."

Dante led me up one more flight of stairs and said, "This is what I really wanted to show you." The third floor of the building was wide open and sunny, with banks of windows, high ceilings and exposed brick walls.

"I want to remodel this into a loft apartment. I'd like this to be our home, Charlie. What do you think? Try to envision it with hardwood floors, a stainless steel kitchen, a big open living area...."

It was empty except for a few pieces of construction equipment, some lumber and a couple piles of palettes. But it was so easy to imagine a beautiful apartment in this big, sunny space. I took him in my arms and said, "I can totally see it. This place is absolutely wonderful."

"I'm so glad you like it." He kissed me again, then pulled back and looked at me with a hint of nervousness. "Want to help me christen our new home?"

"How do we do that, exactly?"

He took my hand and led me across the room. On the floor behind the stacks of palettes was a king-size mattress with crisp white sheets and fluffy pillows, and a bottle of champagne in a silver ice bucket with two glasses beside it.

I laughed at that. "So you've brought me here to seduce me."

"Well, not exactly." He sank down on a corner of the mattress and looked up at me. "I've brought you here so *you* can seduce *me*."

I knelt beside him. "What do you mean?"

"I mean I want you to fuck me, Charlie."

"But, you don't do that."

"I know. But I want to give this to you. I know you've never topped, and I want you to get to experience what it's like to be inside another man."

"What brought this on?"

"I've been thinking about it for a long time. The way we have sex is totally according to my rules, my formula. That may be the only way *I* can fuck, but that's not the only way we can have sex."

"Are you sure about this? You seem nervous."

"Giving up control isn't something I do easily. Or, you know, at all. But I love and trust you, Charlie. So, if you think you want this, I'm prepared to give myself to you."

"Dante," I murmured, and kissed him deeply. I pushed him onto his back on the mattress, laying partly on top of him, and kept kissing him as I ran a hand down his hard, strong body. He remained uncharacteristically passive, resting his hands on my waist.

I pulled off my clothes and stripped him slowly, watching his reactions, trying to gauge whether he was enjoying or merely enduring it. His cock was semi-hard, but his expression was wary. I kissed him again, then sat back on my heels and looked down at him. "This isn't you, Dante."

"I really do want this. I want you to fuck me."

"I want that, too. But you don't have to be so passive. This doesn't have to be sweet and romantic, either. That's not how we fuck."

Dante sat up and considered that for a moment before saying, "You may have a point there." He grabbed me and flung me on my back on the mattress, then climbed on top of me and kissed me savagely.

Instantly, desire spiked within me, and I grabbed him in a rough embrace as he rolled over, pulling me on top of him. He grabbed my ass with both hands as I ground my cock against his and shoved my tongue down his throat, and he thrust up underneath me.

We rolled over again, and I bit his shoulder as he fumbled around under the edge of the mattress, finally coming up with a little bottle of lubricant. "You really planned ahead," I grinned.

He chuckled a little and tossed the bottle to me. "I did. No fucking way was I doing this without lube."

We sat up, kind of straddling each other, his thighs over mine and his legs spread. I tangled my fingers in his hair, pulled him to me and claimed his mouth with a hard kiss, then reached down and took hold of his cock just as he took hold of mine. As we began jerking each other off, I asked, "You ever been fucked, Dante?"

He laughed and said, "Hell no. Who besides you would I ever let do that to me?"

"You ever had anything in you?" I flipped the little bottle of lube open with one hand.

"No. But I think I'm about to." He grinned at me as I drizzled the clear liquid over his cock and balls, making sure plenty was running between his legs. He let go of my cock for a moment and ran his palm over his slick shaft to pick up some lube, then went back to stroking me.

I grinned too, jerking his now slick cock with one hand while reaching between his legs with the other. I leaned down and took his nipple in my mouth and sucked it, then bit down a little as the tip of my finger found his opening and pushed inside.

He laughed again. "Interesting distraction technique, biting me so I don't notice the...ahhhhh," he moaned as I twisted my finger and pushed it deep inside him.

"Less talking, more moaning," I said with a grin as I pumped his cock and crooked my finger inside him, looking for his prostate. It was pretty damn obvious when I found it, his back arching as he grabbed onto me with his free hand.

"Holy shit," he gasped.

"Good?"

"So fucking good."

I fingered him for a while as I licked and bit his earlobe, and then worked a second finger into him. "Oh fuck," he murmured, thrusting his ass onto my hand, and I finger fucked him until I felt him open up.

I pulled out and tipped him back onto his elbows, his thighs still over mine, and grabbed the lube, kind of making a mess with it as I shook with anticipation. I lubed my cock and positioned the tip at his opening, and looked him in the eye. Dante grinned at me and said, "I can't believe we're doing this."

"It was your idea." I was grinning too. "This is your last chance to back out."

"Hell no. Fuck me, Charlie."

I winked playfully and said, "Yes sir." Eyes locked with his, I eased my cock into his body. He grunted and gritted his teeth, but he wasn't about to cry out. Not that tough guy.

I slid into him with one long, slow push, then held still for a moment. When I saw some of the tension in his shoulders ease, and once he let out a long exhale, I started moving in him. It felt amazing. His warm, tight hole milked my cock as I thrust into him. I tried to go slowly and give him time to adjust. But Dante dropped onto his back and grabbed my ass with both hands, pulling me into him. Message received. I started pounding him, hard, and he murmured, "Fuck yes," as he reached between us and stroked his cock with one hand, the other hand still firmly gripping my ass.

As much as I wanted to make it last, it just felt too damn good to hold out for long, and after just a few minutes I announced, "Oh God, I'm gonna cum." I pumped Dante's hole almost violently, crying out as I shot into him.

"Fuck yes Charlie, cum in me," he ground out, rocking his hips up off the mattress to meet my thrusts, drawing every last drop from my balls.

When I was spent, Dante grabbed me in his arms, rolled us over so he was on top of me and kissed me hungrily. I was still inside him. My hands slid to his gorgeous ass as he began to lick and nibble my neck and shoulder. He slid down my body, which pulled my cock out of his little hole, and sucked and bit my nipples until they were hard. He was wasting no time revving me right back up again.

Dante grabbed the lube and poured it over his fingers, then slid his middle finger inside me to the last knuckle, so he was cupping my ass with the rest of his hand. I made that embarrassing sound that happened sometimes, almost a purr, as I wiggled my ass on his hand, and Dante grinned and said, "Good kitty." My laugh turned into a moan of pleasure when he started finger fucking me roughly.

He handed me the lube and said, "Here, hold this." Then he jumped up and pulled me to my feet, and I yelped in surprise as he lifted me onto his shoulder in a fireman's carry. I grinned as I said, "It never ceases to amaze me that you can actually lift me."

"You're not heavy, angel," he told me as he crossed the big open loft with me.

"Maybe not to you."

He'd brought me over to a construction site at one end of the space, and paused to survey the lumber and equipment. "So many options," he said. I could hear the smile in his voice. He slapped my ass, and my cock jumped.

In the next moment, he was bending me over the long feeder table that sat beside a circular saw. It was at the just the right height, jutting my ass up into the perfect fucking position. He went around to the other side of the table and unplugged the saw, then used the power cord to quickly bind my hands together before tying them to a support in the center of the table. "God yes," I murmured as he tied me off securely.

He crouched down right in front of me and I raised my head up and saw that his dark eyes were sparkling with excitement and anticipation. His kiss was surprisingly tender. He pulled back a couple inches and brushed my hair back from my face as he said, "I love you so much, Charlie."

"I love you too, Dante." Then I added with a grin, "I can't wait to see what you do to me."

He smiled at me and stood up, then wound his fingers in my hair and tilted my head up. "This, for starters," he said, and slipped his cock between my lips.

I sucked him eagerly as he slowly fucked my face, my lips wrapped around his thick shaft, the taste of his precum on my tongue. I let out a long, "Mmmmmm." He increased the force of his thrusts a little, and God it was hot. It felt so dirty. So perfect.

I made a little sound of disappointment when he pulled out of my mouth. Dante crouched down so he was at my eye level again and took the lube that was clutched in my hand. He kissed me, then smiled at me as he caressed my cheek with the back of his fingers.

My cock throbbed as he walked around to my ass. He picked something up and ran it down my spine, then slid it over my shoulder where I could see it as he said, "This could be fun." It was an old-fashioned wooden yardstick.

"Oh fuck yes," I moaned, every part of my body tingling with excitement.

Dante paused for a long moment, caressing my exposed ass with the yardstick. I went crazy with desire, squirming and writhing and begging him to beat me, my cock straining.

The first strike was always the best, because I never quite knew when it was coming. Finally, Dante brought the yardstick down across my ass, hard, and I yelled as sensation shot through every part of me, my cock throbbing in response. I widened my stance, making myself more exposed to him, giving him all of me.

He took his time, administering a wonderfully thorough spanking while I yelled and writhed and thrust my hips. Right when I thought I was going to cum just from all of that sensation, he set the yardstick down beside me. I heard a flip-top being opened, and then I felt the incredibly erotic sensation of a cool stream of lube being slowly poured down between my butt cheeks. I moaned and rocked my hips, absolutely desperate for what was going to happen next.

Dante took hold of his big cock and ran the tip up and down my crack, coating it with lube. Then with one hard thrust, he mounted me. "Oh fuck yes," I yelled as he impaled me, taking me so deep that his balls were pressed against my ass. He held still for a long moment while I panted and struggled and begged shamelessly for him to take me, fuck me, fill me with his cum. I felt as if my entire life depended on him thrusting into me. I was that aroused, that totally on edge.

He began fucking me, hard, slamming into my spanked ass, and the pain only amplified the pleasure. He was absolutely pounding me, the big wood and metal table beneath me rocking and creaking as it absorbed some of the force of his thrusts. And then I was cumming, so hard that stars actually popped and swirled in my vision. My cum practically tore from me, shooting all over the underside of the table, spraying across the sawdust-covered floor. Again and again I came, yelling incoherently, fucking myself onto Dante's cock as I thrust back wildly.

In the next moment he was yelling too, his fingers digging into my hips, pulling me back to meet his thrusts, trying to take me as deeply as he possibly could as he shot into me. "Oh God yes, Dante," I mumbled.

When he finally stilled, I was trembling, sweat-drenched, aftershocks of that incredibly intense orgasm making my body practically convulse. The only sound was our jagged breathing in the quiet of what would one day be our home. Dante released my hips and gently massaged the fingerprints he'd left on my body as he slowly eased his cock out of me.

I was glad he still had some energy left, because I was pretty much a quivering mound of jelly at that point. He untied me, came back around the table and scooped me up in his arms, cradling me against his chest. He brought me back to the mattress and laid down with me, holding me against his powerful body.

As I snuggled against his chest, I murmured, "Where'd the mattress come from?"

He chuckled at that. "I had it delivered from my furniture store a couple days ago." He kissed the top of my head.

"What happened to the frame and box spring?"

"The freight elevator's out, and they couldn't get them up the stairs."

I grinned as I nestled into his arms. "You totally planned out your own seduction."

He smiled and said, "I didn't just get the mattress for today. I think it'll be fun to spend the night here occasionally while the loft is being constructed. There's plenty of privacy every night, once the workers go home. And no roommates."

"Mmm, good thought," I whispered as sleep closed in on me. "This is going to be a wonderful home for us. Thank you."

"Thank you too, angel."

"What are you thanking me for?"

"For making me happier than I ever thought possible. I love you so much, Charlie."

"Love you too, Dante," I murmured. "Can't wait to spend forever with you."

****

Christopher's story continues,
and Charlie and Dante get married in
In Pieces
Book Three in the Firsts and Forever Series

For more information on author
Alexa Land or this series,
please visit
http://alexalandwrites.blogspot.com/

Made in the USA
Middletown, DE
12 December 2015